AERIE
Outcast

By Sophie Yao

SOCIETY OF YOUNG INKLINGS

Cover and Interior Illustration: Shu Yao
Interior Design and Composition: Beth Spencewood
Printed in the USA
First Printing: November 2022
ISBN: 978-1-956380-22-4

For all my ornithophile friends

With special thanks to Ms. Melody Reed and Ms. Tasslyn Magnusson

Table of Contents

Part I
Swiftwing, the Philippine Eagle

Part II
Browntuft, the Philippine Hawk-Eagle

Sophie Yao

Map of the Philippines

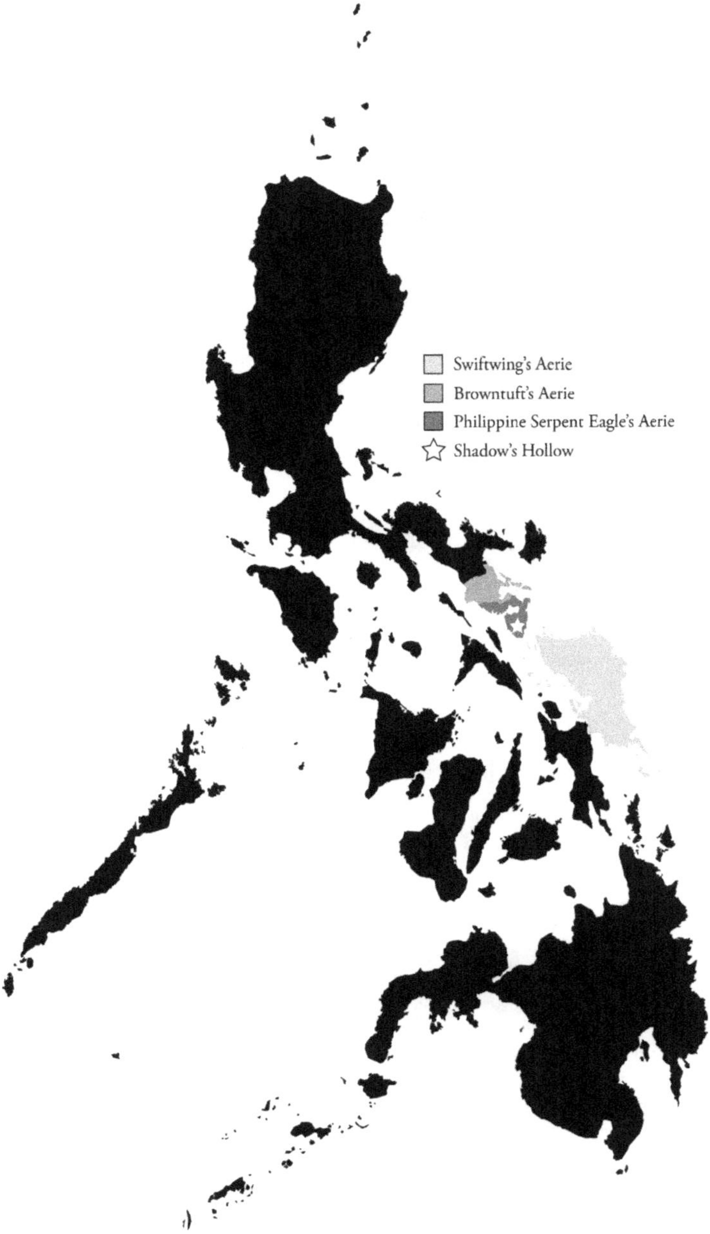

Sophie Yao

Part I

Swiftwing the Philippine Eagle

CHAPTER I

THE CHOOSING

I flapped my wings, shaking them out. Today was the day—the Choosing—when all the eaglets two years old would be chosen to be a Hunter, Warrior, or Healer. My crest fluffed up in agitation, mottling and blending the brown and white as the feathers moved. My life would be decided in the next moments!

The Leader of my Aerie, Keeneye, watched the gathering crowd. She was fifteen years old, which was quite old for a Leader. She had been chosen at age ten as a Hunter, though she didn't hunt much anymore. I watched her tower over me. Even from this distance she radiated a sense of boldness and confidence that I could never hope to have. She would be the one to run the Choosing.

"Slowbird," sneered a voice next to me.

"Sharpbeak," I said, acknowledging the older eaglet's comment. "And why, exactly, am I a slowbird?" For a moment, Sharpbeak, with his cold eyes, faltered. Then he regained stride.

"You see," he started to say, "that I am already a Warrior. Sorry for you, but it's still a few hours until your Choosing. Slowbird." He was only one year older than me, but he always assumed that it was a lot.

I was in a nest about fifty wingspans above the forest floor. I could hear monkeys chittering, but I couldn't hunt yet so I left them alone. The ground far below was wet and dark, and I shuddered at the thought of setting talons there.

I scratched the reddish-brown bark beneath my feet. It was littered with leaves and the remains of prey, like small bones, and was enclosed on all sides by branches that reached up, giving the platform shade and making it cool. And Sharpbeak was here! On my family's platform!

I couldn't help thinking that Sharpbeak looked common—though

I would never say it—while I had dappled white spots on the start of my blue-gray beak. I glared at Sharpbeak. I could never act this way towards my superiors, but Sharpbeak wasn't *exactly* mine . . . right?

"So what?" I snarled. "I'm younger than you. Can't blame me." I imagined what would happen if I said this to my Leader.

"Yeah, I can," said Sharpbeak, much to my annoyance. "You were a weakling . . . you couldn't get out of your shell!" I opened my beak to reply, then realized that I didn't have a snarky comment to make. I narrowed my eyes at Sharpbeak, but turned away.

The male bird puffed out of his feathered chest, then flew to another nest.

There was a Philippine Eagle the same age as me in the nest Sharpbeak had just flown too, but I didn't recognize him. He had dark gray spots under his eyes, and his wings tips had more white on them than other birds. He reminded me of Sharpbeak . . .

I flew towards the clearing, waiting for the Choosing to start. As they say, "The early Eagle catches the civet." Suddenly, a wing brushed my torso.

"Hi, Swiftwing." I turned around and saw my sibling, part of my brood. Her name was Lightfeather, but she was two years older than me. Luckily for me, Lightfeather was way nicer than Sharpbeak, and treated me like an equal. In times like this though, she would start bragging. I landed on a nearby, non-nested tree. My mother, Darktail, soon landed next to me.

"Nice to see you," said Lightfeather. "Listen—Father's a famous Warrior, Mother's a Healer, and I'm a sort-of famous Warrior, so you'd better try to be one!" She playfully hit me with her wing, which had speckled gray-brown dots on the underside.

"And if I don't," I started.

Darktail twitched her tail at me playfully.

"Oh, you will," said Mother. "You're already quite good at flying."

"Thanks," I said. Then the caws began.

The caws symbolized the start of the Choosing. Generally, the Choosing would start from the oldest to youngest. In the Year of the Philippine Eagle, when the egg-laying would start, twenty-five eggs had been laid since there were one hundred fifty some eagles in the Aerie. I was the twenty-fifth eaglet, the youngest. I started to pant. My heart thundered in my chest.

I shivered, and Lightfeather looked at me. "Well, we'd better go. Good luck." She flew to the tree in the center of the clearing, and I followed her.

The caws stopped, and were replaced by a higher-pitched cry. This went on for another five heartbeats, and the oldest eaglet, an eaglet called Goldbelly, half flapped, half stumbled his way to the large platform. It was halfway off the ground in the first fork in the tree. It was made of red bark, leaves, and twigs. Goldbelly was just two moons older than me, but he was on the smaller side. He sat in front of the Leader, his wings thrown carelessly at her feet.

It was obvious Keeneye was trying hard not to grimace. She stared at the young eaglet. He glared back. His eyes were a very pale gray, like a storm just starting, unlike mine, which were a far darker gray-blue, a trait I was proud of.

"Your name?" asked Keeneye.

"Goldbelly." His caw was surprisingly deep. It rang around the clearing in the forest.

"Parents?"

He told her his parents' names. I thought that he would tremble, but he only stared at her fiercely. I would have trembled. Well, maybe not, but my voice at least might have quavered. Traditionally, you announced the father first. I found myself shivering, even though it wasn't cold. My crest fluffed up, and my talons raked the branch until it was almost no more.

"Good,"said Keeneye, dipping her head. She passed her wing over Goldbelly's torso. Legend had it, if the Leader was good and the Ibon[1] Spirit was pleased with the Leader, the Leader would be gifted with interpreting things that other birds couldn't, like right now.

"Goldbelly. You will be a…" The crowd inhaled a breath. They exhaled as she opened her beak to continue. "A Healer."

For a moment, there was silence. Then the cries of happiness split the air. Goldbelly's parents rushed to talk to their son.

This continued. Eaglet to eaglet. The only noticeable ones I really heard were the names I knew. The one that I saw earlier, the one that Sharpbeak confronted, turned out to be called Tawnytop, and was Sharpbeak's younger brother. He became a Warrior like his brother. No surprise there. He was the fifteenth in line.

Sixteen to Twenty-four passed quickly. I took a deep breath.

---

1   Ibon means bird in Tagalog.

My heartbeat quickened, and I tapped my talons on the floor anxiously, ruffling my wings and then tucking them in. Involuntarily, my crest fluffed up and then went down. What would happen if I messed up, and I broke tradition? Then I would die!

As the call rang out, "Twenty five!"

I walked forward along the branch, taking care to fold my wings in, pull my shoulders back, and keep my head high. After choosing twenty-four other Philippine Eagles, I could tell Keeneye was bored. But when she saw me acting all regal, she perked up. Inside, I was screaming and shuddering. But I didn't show it.

I ascended the platform. Her beak opened and closed. I was so excited; I could barely hear the words she said. But after watching the previous Choosings, I knew what to say back.

"Name?"

"Swiftwing." A flicker of recognition passed over the Leader's face. It was no mystery as to why. My father, a Warrior, was practically a living legend. He was an amazing Warrior and in the inner circle of Keeneye's Advisors.

"Parents?"

"Fierceheart, Warrior. Darktail, Healer." Keeneye nodded. I didn't even need to tell her who my parents were since she already knew, but it was tradition. Just as being one of my parent's roles was tradition. The legends of birds that broke the tradition were few and far between.

"Yes." She dipped her head. Then she passed her wing over my own. I could feel the coarse feathers as she touched me, and then what felt like a shock. I was frozen for a moment; my muscles stiff, my beak clenched tight. Then it passed.

Keeneye opened her beak, already framing the word *Warrior*. I opened my beak a little, waiting for the cheers to come as she said the word that would decide my life. Then her face contorted. She clenched her beak together, and then opened it to say the word. What was happening? All my worries came back, stronger than ever.

The word that came out of her mouth wasn't *Warrior* or *Healer*. The word that decided my fate was *Hunter*.

§　　§　　§

Everything was chaos after I broke tradition. Most birds jumped up, scattering feathers and flying to their nest. Others screamed out to the morning sun that was barely showing above the canopy. The sun was blotted out with the flapping of Eagles' wings, and the forest was momentarily plunged into darkness, until the Eagles scattered. The trees were filled with flashes of green and brown and white, and I could hardly see. Surprisingly, the Leader kept silent.

"Swiftwing! Just keep calm!" I heard Darktail screeching and she started to fly towards me. A few other birds hit her out of the way, and I lost sight of her in the melee.

"Mother!" I shouted, only to see her brown and white head pop out of the crowd, her crest up.

A lot of birds, after they realized that squawking around was useless, settled down. I panted in fear, and backed away from Keeneye and the crowd. I raised my crest, trying to look bigger.

"Please," I whimpered. "Am I going to be cast out?" Cast out . . . every Aerie bird's nightmare. They would be living on their own. And now, that might just happen to me.

Keeneye surveyed the crowd with a calm eye. Her feathers were distinctly ruffled, but she stared at the gathering.

"Swiftwing, daughter of Fierceheart, Warrior, and Darktail, Healer, you are hereby exiled from your Aerie." The words rang across the clearing. Silence fell over the place. Keeneye was avoiding my eye, staring down at her talons. I wished that I could fly away already, but I didn't even know how to hunt, and I couldn't survive if I didn't know how.

This matter was addressed when she looked up and caught my eye. "But it would be cruel to leave her as a loner without the skill to hunt."

I realized what she was saying, but it was too much to ask. This could just be something to get my hopes up, then push them down again. One last punishment.

But she went on, and my hopes rose even higher. "So she will be allowed one more day to train to hunt and fight. "

Screams and cries that echoed through the still forest. Finally, another Advisor in the inner circle of Keeneye's, who was also the sworn enemy of my father, snarled, "That is a break of tradition!"

"Aerie at attention!" she shouted. Now an eerie silence fell over the group. They watched me with unblinking eyes. Then Keeneye clucked impatiently, and their attention went to her.

"As I was saying," she said impatiently, "we'll let Swiftwing stay for one day *only*. Then she'll be banished. From this time forward, you will address her as 'Outcast'." When the Leader next spoke, it was with tremor in her voice.

"And if you see her in our Aerie afterwards—" She faltered, staring at Father.

He sat there, unconcerned, looking arrogant and completely fine, which fooled everyone but me, and Lightfeather. I knew that inside, he was a minefield of anger, fear, and sadness.

"Kill her."

It was as simple as that. Those few words held more power than most intricately long sentences do. I whimpered and cowered as birds glared and rasped at me.

No, no, no, no, no. This could not be happening. I was an Advisor's daughter. This had never happened before; why would it happen now? Then I saw my sister shoving her way through the crowd, and suddenly, I felt hope.

Lightfeather flew up to land on the stage. "Leader," she said, crouching down as if she were about to take flight, except that her wings were tucked in. "Swiftwing has done nothing wrong. Perhaps the Ibon Spirit likes her, perhaps it doesn't—" That was all it took to set Keeneye off again. She leaned down, and I could hear her snap at Lightfeather in a harsh rasp.

"Do you think I want to do this? I'm one of the birds in this Aerie that actually likes Swiftwing! She's smart, strong, and, yes, swift, like her name, too!" Well, of course it was too much to think she liked me because of my sunny personality. If I even had any, that was. I guessed that I was pretty swift, though I'd never used swiftness for hunting, since I always assumed that I would be a Warrior. Then, in a louder voice, Keeneye said, "Exactly! The Ibon Spirit may dislike her! We can't have somebird that the Ibon Spirit may find disruptive in our Aerie. Stop protesting. It can't be changed."

Lightfeather stopped, an expression of hope frozen on her face. Then it slowly melted, and she flew to Father, who took her under his wing, even though Lightfeather was already too big for that. She was shaking and muttering to herself.

Keeneye inclined her head toward me. It wasn't really a bow, more like a nod of acknowledgement. She sighed to herself, then said to me, in a low rasp, "I really don't want to do this. But you have to understand that if I let you stay, I would probably have a mutiny on my wings. And the Aerie would probably win."

She could let me stay . . . but I knew the role of leadership didn't come easily. In times like this, she would have to pick the Aerie's choice.

"Fine," I said. "I want to try living as an outcast! Why not?" I couldn't believe I had said that. Keeneye glared at me, then signaled with her wing that the Choosing was over. The crowd dispersed, leaving me with my family.

I shared almost no words with Father or Mother. They could see that I didn't want to talk. Instead, they only wrapped their wings around my torso. Then we shared prey until the sun was setting.

Even when I should have been sleeping, I was still awake, staring at the stars that dotted the night sky.

CHAPTER 2

TRAINING

The next day I had a lump in my heart, and it was the worst in my short life.

My lesson with Scarletcrest, my Warrior trainer who was eight years my senior, went by quickly. I could hardly concentrate when I met her; the leaves were too bright, the small bird chirps too loud. She was waiting for me when I arrived on the designated platform—and then, she fell off backwards.

I was screaming my throat hoarse—when I thought to look at

where she fell, and saw that she had just saved herself in the nick of time. She was hard to see, because of the way the bright red leaves blended in with her crest. Scarletcrest was doing some cool twists and turns, and then she landed on my platform again. Her beak was twisted in a smirk. "That's how you fly," she sneered. "Even a Hunter should do that."

I didn't think I could, so I said, "That's impossible, Scarletcrest! You can't expect me to do that!" Luckily, she wasn't Keeneye, so at least I could exclaim in her presence. I was pretty sure she was expecting me to say yes and to start training right away. The smug look on her sharp face disappeared, and was replaced by one of disapproval.

"Number one," she said, "you will always address me as '*Warrior Scarletcrest*'. Two, that's not even half of it. We'll still be learning how to fight. And three, *never throw your talons up in the air before you try!*" Her last words were screeched into my face.

"Okay!" I screeched back, galvanized into action. I jumped off the platform, and started flying. Instinctively, I was soaring. Scarletcrest flew next to me.

"No!" she shrieked at me, hitting my wing with her own. The sudden change of symmetry moved me, and I found myself flipping over in the air, falling at the same time. I righted myself just in time, as I was about to hit a tree branch, and soared back to the platform where Scarletcrest was waiting. How had she gotten there so quickly?

"We're going to learn the simple slash," she said, and demonstrated the movement.

I copied her, my talons whistling through the air.

"Not bad. Now, the jab."

"What?" I asked. "You jab someone with your words? 'You're small?' Like that?"

"No!" she screamed angrily. "Like this!" She curled her claws in and jabbed me in the chest with her talon.

"Ouch!" I bent my claws in and tried to jab her in the chest, only to have her lean to the side. My talon went through the air next to her head, and she batted it aside.

"Practice that later," she snapped. "Now aerial attacks. Go." I was on my wings in an instant.

She grabbed me by the talons, and then was spinning me around upside down until I felt like I might fall off. The wind rushed past my feathers, and the blood pumping through my veins was louder than ever. Then she let go and I was flying towards a tree. "Dodge!" she screeched.

The only thing I could do was twitch my tail before I slammed into the tree.

She glared down at me, her beak twisted in contempt. "That was," she started, "horrible."

With that, she jumped up and flew away.

§ § §

At the end of my lesson with Brazenclaw, Scarletcrest's brother who also happened to be my Hunter trainer, we went out for a real, free-style hunt, at the edge of the Aerie, near the sea.

We flew into the forest away from the Aerie, and I started practicing flying, grabbing my prey, a bat, mid-flight, and lunging at flying lemurs while their backs were turned.

A golden macaque was hanging on a vine, swinging lazily to and fro.

"Go!" said Brazenclaw.

I flapped the tips of my wings softly, pointing my beak at the monkey. I got my talons ready, pointing them up and out. As soon as I was less than a wingspan away, I flapped hard and slammed my talons into the monkey's back. It twitched once then fell limp.

"You have an amazing aim," Brazenclaw said. "You shoot out your talons, and never fail to kill your prey." That was stretching it. I'd failed to kill a lot of bats because they moved around so much.

"Sorry," Brazenclaw said, and he did actually look sorry. "But you've already learned everything I can teach you. One last good-bye, and then you're an outcast forever."

I wanted to collapse. I knew that my time in the Aerie was coming to an end, but it had passed so quickly. Brazenclaw was already saying good-bye.

"Bye," I choked out. "May the wind follow you wherever you go." That was a farewell that was traditional to the Philippine Eagles. Well, as far as I knew, it was traditional to all the birds in the Philippines. Popular legends talked about other raptors in other places across the Great Blue, where the farewells were "May you talons be ever sharp."

"Well," said Brazenclaw, obviously hoping to cheer me up, "you know, we could have one more round of hunting. One more flight—"

"No."

"This way," said Brazenclaw, looking subdued. "Dive, let me see you one last time."

We both dove, but all of a sudden, a huge tree seemed to appear in front of me. It was huge, and the bark was rough, with green leaves and brown bark that I was about to smash into. Brazenclaw clumsily swooped out of the way, and it wrenched my heart as I realized that it had been planned. I tried to dodge the tree trunk, angling my wings to catch the wind, but it was blowing me into the tree and I smashed into it. A wave of blackness crashed over me.

The last thing I saw was Brazenclaw winging away.

CHAPTER 3

BROWN STALKER

I woke up scared.

For some reason, this feeling of dread welled up somewhere in me. I felt strangely empty, and wanted to shriek. Hollowness and loss penetrated my insides. Everywhere I looked, shadows that had seemed relatively harmless now looked like they held a monster inside. Instinctively, I moved out of the way. A small sapling could conceal an enemy in its boughs. Fear overwhelmed me and I tucked my head under my wing, wanting to give up. Then a sudden feeling that took away the fear washed over me—

But first, I felt my aching head with my wing. The feathers and crest were flattened. For a moment, I wondered why I wasn't in my nest, and then flashbacks came. The Choosing. Break of tradition. Flying into a tree. What had happened after that? I had probably fallen from the tree. I opened my eyes. As I had expected, I was on the ground, staring up at the forest canopy. I felt small and insignificant. Philippine Eagles were the biggest Eagles, but right now, I felt puny.

I inspected my wings and body. A few small scratches from when the bark had scraped me, and a few loose feathers, but other than that, I was fine.

Brazenclaw . . . I was angry. That had definitely been a setup. No one could have dodged it if they weren't ready, but Brazenclaw, a Hunter, had managed to avoid the branch.

Betrayal.

Obviously.

I wanted to scream. I wanted to kill something, preferably not a bird, but my mind was still so angry at Brazenclaw. How could he?

And I thought he was nice. Well, it turned out, no one in my Aerie was trustworthy! I hadn't even said good-byes to my family yet!

Still, I had more pressing matters to think about. Less past, more present. At least I could hunt. And fight. But first, I needed to see if I could even get up.

I got up and was instantly overcome by a wave of dizziness. I shook myself out, preening all the dirt and gummy sap-paste out of my wings and body. I felt around for a rising draft of air, and used it to fly up the tree trunk. I started to feel far better. The fear earlier dissipated. I thought I would die right away, but instead, I actually had a chance of living.

§   §   §

In this forest, raptors marked their territory by scratching a few lines in the big trees in their territory. The marks were always made at the first sideways branch. Soon I found the scratches. The Philippine Eagle's ones were just a simple diagonal cross, because we were one of the more important tribes and needed no complications. Other, more diverse species, had really complicated symbols. The scratches on the tree were still the

Philippine Eagle's, but as I started working my way away from the Aerie, north, they started changing.

Territories usually had a free space in between them. Well, other than the narrow seas. A little after the shore of the narrow seas, until the beach gave way to trees, was unclaimed territory. To mark that free space, the marks were mixtures of the other groups of birds.

I recalled my lessons. My trainers sometimes said throwaway comments like, "We are surrounded by the Changeable and Philippine Hawk-Eagles and Philippine Serpent Eagles." The Changeable Hawk-Eagle's mark had two diagonal, parallel lines. The Philippine Serpent Eagle's had two vertical, parallel lines. That meant the horizontal cross was probably the Philippine Hawk-Eagle's.

I tucked my wings under my breast. My name was Outcast now. If someone asked me, and I replied "Outcast," I would probably be the subject of a joke. But I shouldn't argue with the Ibon Spirit's choice.

I stopped flying, and landed on a tree marked with a horizontal cross with a diagonal slash, and surveyed my surroundings. The forest here was far different from my former Aerie's one. It was unfamiliar, but still looked similar. The beach was up ahead, with its shining white sand and clear blue waters. They were beautiful and turquoise, with the white sand underneath showing through. The vastness of the sea ahead made me want to turn back. I took a deep breath, then launched myself at the waters.

It was a while before I landed on the beach on the other side, my talons digging into the soft grains. I glanced at the waters behind me, then jumped off and continued gliding.

Changeable Hawk-Eagles and Philippine Serpent Eagles both were hostile towards Philippine Eagles, and might attack me. But Philippine Hawk-Eagles sometimes allied with Philippine Eagles when a greater threat rose up, like floods or Human disturbances.

I was going to need a place to drink first. I could feel my throat getting drier and drier, and when out of the corner of my eye I saw a glint of light blue, I started flying to it.

It wasn't much. Just a small puddle from where water dripped from a leaf. But I landed on the floor and leaned forward and dipped my beak in the warm water. It tasted like dirt, very much unlike the spring-fed pool of fresh water near the Aerie.

However, it quenched my thirst a little, but I would have to find a stream or lake later. For now, it was enough.

I looked up at the nearest tree, and flew halfway up. The unclaimed territories were usually pretty big, about three tall trees' height from one side to the other. The reason why there were free spaces was so that you could think over, *Do I really want to go in here?* Or, *Do I really want to leave there?*

Well, I didn't really have a choice. Keeneye had said that if I was seen on Philippine Eagle territory, I would be killed, and I didn't want to be killed. I still had thirty-five more years of life, if I could survive this.

This part of the forest was really unfamiliar. Trees grew closer, so I wished I had listened to Scarletcrest every time I narrowly missed a tree. Once, I got tangled in a vine and thrashed around before I realized that it was harmless. I slowly untangled myself, my crest raised in embarrassment as I imagined Warriors, swooping through the tight-knit forest with ease, flipping over and dodging artfully.

The sun was sinking. It was dusk now. I had been flying for a very long time, and since I wasn't used to flying, I was exhausted. I found myself following the schedule back in the Aerie. Dusk meant food, and so I hunted a flying fox, which was a bat that had a head that looked like a fox's.

I waited, standing halfway up a tree in the large fork, until there was a rustle of movement and a small shape flew out of the adjacent tree and landed on mine. Then my talon flew out and slashed across its throat.

I flew three-quarters up a tree to rest. I was okay at making stick-nests, but there wasn't any time, and I could sleep just fine standing up on branches.

I devoured the flying fox. It was okay, but I would still have to hunt in the morning. With that in mind, I closed my eyes and drifted off to sleep.

§   §   §

I opened my eyes, the sun's rays filtering through my eyelids. I tried to remember what had happened. I tried to remember why I was on an unclaimed territory tree, when I was part of the Aerie. It had been almost a moon now that I'd been away from the Aerie, perfecting my hunting and attacking skills, and staying in the same place.

Now, I started heading north. As long as there were no birds to act as obstacles, I should get to the Philippine Hawk-Eagles by noon. If there were obstacles, I could only hope for the best.

My morning was relatively clear, until I heard rustling in the bushes underneath me. I looked down, but there was nothing. Not even a feather. Satisfied that it was only the wind, I moved on. But then the leaves in a tree moved. I whirled around and flapped the corner of my wings. I almost fell out of the air. Nothing there. Again. I had a sick feeling that something— *or someone* was trailing me. But if it was an enemy, I would have been attacked by now.

I continued my flight. Every so often, I would whirl around to try to catch my stalker unprepared. Leaves rustled and fell, but that was just the wind. I tried to pick out movement in the leaves, but could find none. Unfortunately, he or she was amazing at staying out of sight, which told me that it was probably small.

Then there it was again! That telltale rustle of the branches, the loose leaves that fell to the ground. But no sign of a bird. I kept on flying. The trees were denser here, so it would be hard to see my stalker even if they were out in the open. Well, that was a bit of a stretch, but whatever. The tenseness just made me want to give up, tuck my head into my wing and go to sleep.

Finally, fed up with these acrobatics, I landed on a nearby tree and said, "Whoever you are, you can come out now, you know. I won't attack you."

For a moment, there was silence. Then the leaves next to me

moved. Startled, I leapt off the tree branch and only opened my wings to glide just in time. The foliage stopped moving. *Seriously, Swiftwing—Outcast?* I asked myself, *Why did you have to scare it away?*

I flew to the adjacent tree. There! A blur and a small brown shape flashed in my peripheral vision. I blinked and shook my head, feeling nervous and alone. Back in the Aerie, I had been safe. Now I was by myself.

"Sorry I scared you before," I called out quietly. "You can come out."

For a moment, I waited. When there was no answer, I flew around the area. When I saw a dark gray, almost black, shape on the ground, I suddenly dived, and sank my talons into the back of its neck. I turned it around so I could see its face. It was a palm civet. There was good eating on a civet, if you could catch one. They were fast and agile. This one must have been distracted. I grabbed it in my claws and flew back to the same tree I knew my stalker was in. Then I opened my beak and ripped out a chunk of meat and ate it. I nudged it to the leafy foliage to my left, where the mystery bird hid.

"You can have some, you know," I said softly. There was no response. Disappointed, I opened my beak to take another bite. But then suddenly, I heard a sharp intake of breath. And it wasn't mine. I looked at the leaves, and found two dark amber eyes staring into mine.

CHAPTER 4

A FRIEND

The eyes stared back at me. I found myself blinking right back at them. Then the eyes closed, and it was hard to see them again.

Finally, a hoarse voice whispered, "How do I know I can trust you? Flying feathers, you're a..."

I didn't know what to say. I stared into the depths of the leaves. "I'll tell you when you come out," I said. "You can trust me because I'm an outcast. I don't have anything to fight for." I could hear the bitterness in my voice, but I made no attempt to hide it. Not like when I was in the

Aerie. Now I was free.

The leaves moved and created a small gap in the foliage, and I finally saw what my stalker looked like.

It was a male Philippine Hawk-Eagle. He was small for a Hawk-Eagle, which led me to believe that he probably had been thrown out of his Aerie because he was a...well, runt. He had dark brown feathers, and his eyes, which were amber, now I could see them, had gold specks in them. His crest wasn't very tall. He obviously was a juvenile eaglet, maybe around twenty moons old. For a moment, we stared at each other. I could see a glint of malice in his eyes, the way his talons itched to rip through flesh. Or was it just my imagination?

Then he spoke, "Who are you?"

Funny, wasn't it, how this was the second question he asked, when for me, it would always be the first. I glared at him, "Who are you?"

He looked confused now. He looked around, like he was searching for an answer.

"What?" he asked. Then my meaning dawned on him. "Flying feathers, I asked you first!" he said.

I sighed. He got me.

"I'm a Philippine Eagle," I said, and when he opened his beak to point out I hadn't told him my name, I continued, "and I used to be called

Swiftwing, but now my name's now Outcast."

"Flying feathers! Not really," he said. "There's no way your name could actually be Outcast." I fluffed my feathers up.

"Yes, my name is Outcast," I snapped. "Call me Swiftwing if you want, but the Ibon Spirit called me Outcast. Our Leader, Keeneye, said so." The bird stared at me for a moment. He started to preen his chest feathers.

"Flying feathers! You don't know?" he asked softly. Still angry at him for laughing at my changed name, I let my feathers fall down, but didn't look at him when I asked my question.

"I don't know what?" I hissed. "Don't tell me that the Ibon Spirit isn't real or something, because I know it is." The Hawk-Eagle looked horrified and offended, but I didn't care.

"Of course not!" he said, then added, and looked curiously at me, "You don't know that Keeneye was killed?"

§   §   §

It was like my wings had been ripped off and I had been thrown to the ground from thirty wings high. In shock. The wind knocked out of me. Bones broken. Back snapped. Unable to breathe. Near death. Not only that, what would happen to my Aerie, now that their Leader was dead? What would happen to Father and Mother and Lightfeather?

I felt horrified. Then slowly, my suspicious part took over. A part of my brain whispered, *How do you know he's not lying?* Because I didn't. I couldn't, unless the Ibon Spirit somehow helped me, and I had a feeling, due to its latest involvement with the Choosing, it wouldn't. Still, this news rattled me. But I tried not to show it.

"Okay, first, follow me. I feel a little exposed here," I said, and tried to sound all casual, even though my mind screamed, *No! I should go back!* Browntuft looked at me for a short while. I stared back at him.

Then he said, "Okay." We both jumped off the branch and I flew towards a larger tree, and we both landed on a branch covered with foliage.

"Alright. Now we can talk. What's your name, and what do you mean that Keeneye's dead?" I asked.

"Yes?" he asked. "Well, my name's Browntuft, and what do you want to know about your Leader's death?" I clenched my beak together. He knew what I wanted to know. As if reading my thoughts, Browntuft cocked his head to the side, and said, with obvious amusement in his voice, "By whom was she killed, you're probably thinking? The Philippine Serpent Eagles killed Keeneye. I heard from my Leader right before I was cast out."

"But why were you cast out?"

He breathed in. "From what you've heard, does my Aerie sound strong to you?"

"You're small, but I guess," I said, not sure where he was going.

"It's because before every Choosing, the Leader throws out the runts." He started to preen. "Like me. To seem strong, so we won't be attacked."

"Did they at least train you?" I asked, horrified.

"No," he said, cocking his head. "So I can't hunt my food that well. Speaking of which . . ." he cast a meaningful glance at the civet. I, not being a nutbrain, understood what that meant.

I moved the palm civet closer to him, and he started ripping chunks of meat off the carcass. Soon enough, it was almost stripped down to just a few scraps.

"Wow, you must be hungry," I said in surprise. So I *had* been correct about him being thrown out because he was small, just not in the way I imagined. Browntuft nodded. I didn't even know why I had fed him.

"I was," he corrected. "Flying feathers, that palm civet was good."

"I can hunt more," I said, and when he opened his beak to say yes, I quickly added, "But not right now. We eat morning and night." For a moment, I could tell Browntuft was surprised. Maybe because he had a different mealtime. But I wasn't going out of my way to hunt for him early just because he was hungry. He had just eaten almost an entire civet. I had only eaten a large beakful.

Maybe Browntuft realized what I was thinking, because he didn't argue. He only blinked his large, gold flecked amber eyes.

"So?" he asked. I realized he was wondering what we should do. He probably viewed me as the leader, since I was bigger than him. Well, that wasn't too bad. I had never been viewed as a leader before.

"Well," I said, "I need to know how old you are. And can you fight?" As I had suspected, he was twenty-two moons old, but he couldn't fight.

"You know what?" I asked. "We can't keep going anymore. If what you said was true, then they'd probably attack us."

"Who?"

"The Philippine Serpent Eagles," I replied. "Or the Philippine Hawk-Eagles; they turned you away."

His amber eyes fixed on a point behind my head. I started to turn around, but Browntuft hissed, "No. Don't turn around. There's an owl watching us in the tree next to the tree next to us. It's a Philippine Eagle Owl. The biggest one I've ever seen. I think it notices us, but it's making no move toward us." I noticed that while Browntuft was talking, he had looked away from the Owl.

I knew what Eagle Owls were. They were supposed to be really wise and settled many wars. The bigger, the wiser. One was even rumored to be able to understand those little featherless peach-colored things called Humans and talk to them, and they would understand him. The name of the one that knew how had been called Ochrear, and might have been the biggest Eagle Owl anywhere.

"You're kidding!" I said.

Browntuft narrowed his eyes.

"If you don't believe me, see for yourself. But he might kill you. Flying feathers, he's big!" I started to believe him. I had a feeling that this Browntuft didn't lie.

"How big?" I rasped. Browntuft twisted his beak, estimating.

"Well, he's not too big. Maybe a little smaller than you." That was still massive for an Eagle Owl. I wouldn't be surprised if the creature could talk back to Humans. For whether or not he could understand Humans, the answer had to be yes.

"He's moving," Browntuft whispered. "I don't know why he's not sleeping. Maybe we woke him up. Probably. Flying feathers—he flew to the nearby tree. You know, the one next to us." I wanted to look behind me so much, but I knew if I did, that could result in our death. I contented myself by preening. Then, struck by an idea, I pretended to raise my wing to clean it, then peeked under it for a second.

The Eagle Owl was huge. And with his experience, he would probably beat me in a fight. He was the color of tree bark, so his most striking features were his bright yellow eyes with deep red pupils. His talons were long and sharp.

I had seen him mid-flight before I turned back. His wings moved silently. Then I heard the quiet scrape as his talons looked for purchase on the tree next to us. Then another scratch as he jumped up from that tree. There was no other place for him to go.

He headed straight toward us. But Browntuft hadn't been looking when the Eagle Owl landed and took off again, so I was still taken by surprise when a calm and low voice said next to me, "Hello, Swiftwing. Would you like to come to my hollow?"

§   §   §

I'd never heard anything so creepy in my life. His voice was low and dark, like low thunder, and smooth and calm, like a pool. Two things that didn't go together, but the Eagle Owl fitted them perfectly, like two hemispheres of one eggshell. I shuddered, and slowly turned around.

"Who are *you*?" I asked, not believing I was even talking to an Eagle Owl. My first question was that one, of course. No mystery there.

The Eagle Owl squinted his eyes at me, while lifting his beak, making him look like he was smiling. "So that's the first question you ask me?" he said. "Now, listen to mine. Didn't I say to come to the hollow?" There it was. He hadn't been asking me. He had been saying that I had to come.

I looked at Browntuft. He was at a loss for words. So was I. Finally, I gathered my courage, and said, "Do we have to, Eagle Owl?"

The Owl narrowed his eyes at me, except this time, he wasn't trying to smile. "Yes. And call me Shadow." Shadow? Who had given him that name? Then I remembered that his feathers were dark brown like tree bark.

It wouldn't have taken too much imagination to make the name Shadow. I nodded, but Shadow noticed my hesitation. He imitated a smiling Human face. The way he did it— it was just so uncanny. I decided I didn't want this Eagle Owl as an enemy.

"Sure," I said. "As in, I'll-go-to-your-hollow sure."

"Very good." Shadow nodded his head, then, without even turning his body, he revolved his head to look at Browntuft. "And you, Browntuft?"

Browntuft swallowed. I could see his feathered throat move. "Yes," he said quietly. "How do you know our names?"

"Browntuft, he probably just overheard," I said. Then I looked at Shadow for confirmation, but he only made a Human-like coughing sound.

"I'm an Eagle Owl. Eagle Owls are wise," he said quietly. "Don't ask me how." I looked at his long yellow talons and shuddered. I probably shouldn't ask.

"Nice one!" said Browntuft, trying and failing to lighten the mood.

Shadow whipped his head around, scrutinizing Browntuft. Then he moved his head up and down like a Human did when it was nodding.

"You are right. Why are we here, doing small talk, when we could be in my comfortable hollow?"

I wondered if his hollow really was that comfortable. Too many times, Sharpbeak had tricked me by saying, "Oh, this bed of leaves is really comfortable," but when I stepped on it, there were sharp rocks everywhere.

"Yes, it is comfortable, Swiftwing!" said Shadow, like he had read my thoughts.

But I wasn't really surprised. After all, he was an Eagle Owl.

Shadow shook his head from side to side in mock exasperation. "Really, eaglets these days. So untrusting." Since I didn't want to offend him, I dipped my head.

"Okay, so where's the hollow?" I asked, trying to act upbeat.

Shadow fixed me with an uncomfortable stare. I shifted from one talon to the other, nervous. If this was a trap... No, it wasn't good to dwell on such things. If I did, I would never grow in life.

Finally, Shadow nodded. "A good question," he admitted. "As an Eagle Owl, I should have been able to tell right away. Unfortunately, I was a bit distracted with your nutbrained questions. Well, the hollow is on the other side of the tree behind me. Follow me."

And with that, he leapt up from the branch and flew silently away.

CHAPTER 5

THE HOLLOW

Browntuft and I looked at each other. Then Browntuft sighed. "We might as well follow, we can't really fly away over the ocean or anything."

Shadow had been right; his hollow was a prey's throw away and in the tallest tree in the unclaimed area. Three quarters up was a large hole about as tall as me on the outside but as tall as two of me on the inside, filled with bracken and leaves. In the corner, near the edge of the hollow, was a pile of young leaves that probably served as Shadow's bed. It was quite big and I fit inside with enough space to stand up straight and turn around. I imagined living here. I could probably survive, it was big enough. How had Shadow found a place like this? It was a place meant for Leaders, not Eagle Owls. I stared at Shadow, in the hollow. What would he do to us once we were inside?

I tucked in my wings a little and crashed into the floor of the hollow. Browntuft stumbled back from where he had been poking around in the ground, but Shadow didn't seem surprised. He merely nodded at me and backed away.

"Hello," I said. "Learned anything, Browntuft?" Browntuft nodded, now hammering at the walls with his talons.

I walked over to a wall, and saw dark brown scorch marks on it. I tried to ignore Shadow, who was right there, watching me. I didn't want to turn my back on him, or anger him either.

I walked over to the leafy bed and gingerly put my talon on it. The leaves were good. They were soft and springy, and when I bent my knees to let my tail touch it, I felt sleepy. I got out of there before I got any ideas.

"So, what do you think?" I was pretty sure Shadow had been waiting to ask this, because he sounded rather impatient. Just to tease him, I narrowed my eyes and lifted my beak in the air in a smile. "Ha. Very funny," said Shadow. "Now answer!"

Browntuft answered when I was still looking at the walls of the hollow. "It's very big. Twice as tall as you, I noticed. And it's cool that this was made in a fire." He was jittery, and kept moving around, not looking at Shadow or me.

"Yes," said Shadow, sounding proud. But something in his eyes told me that this was an act, and he was bored. So I tried addressing the real and important topic.

"Why are we here?" I asked. Shadow glared blackly at me. His pupils became smaller.

"I just want to talk to you," he said. Since I didn't have a comeback, I just dipped my head at him.

"It's afternoon. Shouldn't you sleep now?" I asked. Legend had it that Owls sleep with their faces down, and I wanted to see somebird so dignified as Shadow sleep in that awkward position.

Shadow looked surprised, probably because he realized I was correct. He seemed a bit more annoyed when he replied, rather gruffly, "It's not my fault I'm awake since you birds woke me up." After that, he promptly walked to his bed, and collapsed facedown.

I wanted to run out right now and escape, but I knew that

Browntuft probably wouldn't be able to follow me for long. He walked over to me, tucking his wings in again. "You know, I think I'm a burden. You can't escape—I mean, go away without me. Maybe go hunting and earn his favor."

I looked at him. Then my mind processed what he had said. "Okay." I walked to the opening in the tree trunk, and gripped the edge with my talons. Leaning forward, I opened my wings outside of the hollow and jumped up from the opening. I extended my wings to glide, then soared higher so I could have more space to fly. Looking down, I could see a small white-and-gray shape on a nearby bough. This would be a perfect place to hunt, the way it was situated. Quiet, unassuming, while you could see all the prey in the glade.

A giant cloud rat, the white-and-gray shape, was alert, looking up at the sky every few heartbeats. When it saw me, it ducked into a hole in the tree I hadn't seen before. I let out a small whine of dismay. I had forgotten that not all hunts ended in success. I had gotten too used to catching my prey every time I started hunting.

Just then, a loud screech came from behind. I whipped around, but it was only Browntuft. He was panting heavily from the long flight, and had a tuft of fur in his right talon.

"I never knew hunting could be so hard before I was cast out," he panted. "But a squirrel just escaped me, and I got a bit of fur." He held up his right talon. The tuft of fur was small, but for somebird only twenty-two moons old and with no lessons, it was pretty impressive.

"That's good!" I said. "Maybe I can teach you to hunt sometime. Then when we—" I looked in the general direction of the hollow, to make sure Shadow couldn't hear us— "escape, we can survive. Or if we get separated."

"So, have you caught anything?" Browntuft asked. I glared at him, and showed him my empty talons.

The sun was setting. In a few minutes, it would be nightfall and Shadow would come looking for us. "We should be getting back to Shadow." Browntuft dipped his head in acknowledgement. He took a deep breath, then launched himself into the sky, flapping until I told him to "extend your wings to glide!" As soon as he did that, I flew after him. It was probably the most fun I had since I had been exiled.

Soon we arrived at Shadow's hollow. Shadow was awake, and he was watching us. The moon's light reflected off his yellow eyes, giving them an ethereal quality. He nodded when we flew into the hollow.

"Don't leave like that again," said Shadow menacingly. "If you do,

I might have to go hunt you down." I shuddered. The idea of an Eagle Owl chasing after us *in the dark* didn't fail to make me feel queasy. I lowered my head in submission.

"Go to sleep now," Shadow snarled. "Seeing as you failed to catch something, I'd better do it. Eat the squirrel."

What squirrel? As far as I could see, there was no squirrel in the hollow. Then the Eagle Owl hooked his sharp talon around a piece of bark that was flaking off and ripped it off. Underneath was a hole about one third of a wing high and one sixth of wing wide. Inside there was a large fat squirrel and another large vole. Shadow took out the squirrel, dropped it on the floor, then sealed the hole in the wall again by jamming the bark in place.

I opened my beak to talk, then thought better about it and closed my beak. It was quite smart, the way Shadow did it, but in my former Aerie, you would deliver prey to the Leader and they would check to make sure it fit well with the family size—for example, two birds couldn't eat an entire monkey, and a family of four needed more than a small squirrel. Then the family would eat the prey right away.

"Doesn't it rot?" I asked.

"Sometimes it does, if you don't eat it soon enough," said Shadow. "But usually, the hole gives it a different taste—it's quite a good one though."

I leaned down and ripped off a bite of the squirrel. The hole must have kept it warm, because it was soft and juicy, and Shadow was correct— it had a different taste about it, like it had absorbed the wood flavor. Holding the squirrel down with my foot, I took another chunk before Browntuft nudged me over with his wing. Then he took two bites.

We alternated eating the squirrel until it was just a few crushed bones and leftover scraps. Shadow took the remains of the animal and threw it out of his hollow. Then he flew out of his hollow, so silently that we didn't notice until we couldn't see him anymore.

I looked at Browntuft, then gestured to the wall. We both walked over to it, leaned on it, then closed our eyes to sleep.

§   §   §

It was morning when I woke up, and instinctively, I looked up, hoping to see Sharpbeak glaring down at me laughing, but I found Browntuft next to me. He was awake, and had a confused expression on his face. I nudged him, and he looked at me. Alarm flashed over his sharp features. Then he slumped down. "Whoops, I forgot," he said. "I thought you were an enemy."

We both looked at Shadow. His bed was empty, but just then, a screech sounded and Shadow flew into the hollow.

"Awake already, are you?" he snapped. "Eat the vole in the hole! I'll be going to sleep now. Don't wake me up!" With that, he stalked over to his bed and laid down. He closed his yellow eyes and started sleeping.

I tried to remember what Shadow had done to open the food-supply hole. I hooked my claw around the flaky bark, and pulled. The bark came off, and I looked inside.

It had been recently filled. Now there were three mice, one vole, and two gophers. Shadow had probably hunted while we were sleeping.

We ate the vole, ripping off the succulent flesh. Now it was our turn to hunt, and since I had promised to teach Browntuft, I held up my talon and pointed to the hole. We both jumped out.

"Extend your wings to glide!" I shouted, but didn't need to tell him. The Hawk-Eagle had instinctively done it from last time, and I screeched with approval. Then I saw a dark brown shape on a bough under us. I fixed my eyesight on it and got closer. I pointed my beak toward it, and Browntuft noticed. I watched as he circled above it. Then he suddenly dived, but he kept on screeching as he did. Finally, he landed near the squirrel and shot out his talon to catch it, but by then, the squirrel had dashed away, and he only hooked a bit of fur and yanked it out. I couldn't believe it. Screeching as he dived? That was crazy! I circled once, then flew down to him, adjusting my wings so I would land right next to him. I felt myself feeling amused, since before, I would have been the inexperienced one. Now, I appeared to be the teacher.

"Listen," I said. "Good aim with your talon at the last second, but make sure you can adjust if your prey tries to run away. Also, don't make noise when you dive. Otherwise your prey gets alerted."

Browntuft looked down at his talons. "Show me," he said, a challenge evident in his voice. I imitated him.

"Show you?" I asked. He nodded. "Watch." I launched myself from the tree I was on and flew to the next one. Three trees away, I could see a giant cloud rat. *Aha. Let's see if you can evade me again.* This time, the cloud rat didn't have a hole to run to. I flew to the next tree. The bark was more slippery, and I almost slipped. I glanced at Browntuft. Luckily, he hadn't seen that, instead, he was staring at the cloud rat.

Then the next tree. If I flew now, when it was alert, I would risk startling the cloud rat. Then I saw it scrabble at the rough tree trunk, the tongue dart out, and I knew it was time. I angled my wings to keep silent, and flew towards the creature. Approaching the target, I increased speed and suddenly sunk my claws into its neck. I flipped it over so I could see its black muzzle, eyes, and neck, and white tail and body. Then I flew back up to Browntuft.

"Wow! That was amazing, Swiftwing!" he said.

"I showed you—!"

"Amazing!"

"I showed you—!"

"Awesome!"

"Browntuft!" I screeched. He stopped praising me, looking rather embarrassed. "Look, I caught it," I said. "See how I hunt? I want you to try that."

Browntuft's eyes widened. He blinked. "I'm not sure," he said doubtfully. "You're older than me and you got trained. But... fine."

"Okay, look for prey," I said.

Browntuft flew to the next tree, but I knew I shouldn't follow him. In short sprints like these, he was a really fast flier, actually. I suspected that he had seen something, because I heard him give a small squeal of excitement. Then he skipped one tree and flew to the next one, before diving to the floor. I notice, with a sense of accomplishment, that he didn't screech as he flew. Suddenly, there were a bunch of yelps and squeals of fear. A few seconds after, Browntuft reappeared, carrying a small mouse in his talons. Not typical eagle food, but Shadow would probably enjoy it as a meal when he woke up—and if he was grumpy, it might make him happier. I nodded, and he was bursting with pride.

"Look, I did it," he said. "A mouse for Shadow, and the cloud rat can be for us."

I looked up at the sun at the word Shadow. It was near the treetops, and it would be sundown soon, so we spent our time hunting. By the end of the day, we had caught one huge squirrel, one small water vole, and another cloud rat. Browntuft had caught the squirrel, just snapping its neck before it could have dashed away. A worthy contribution to the food-supply hole. He had also gotten the water vole. We flew home quickly, not wanting to risk Shadow's anger.

As I entered the hollow second, with a clumsy crash that made Shadow wake up, I noticed Browntuft opening the hole. He shoved his squirrel, vole, and mouse in, and I got up and put my two cloud rats in the hole. Then he sealed it in. In the dusk light, the hollow looked creepier and darker than it had in the morning.

"Thanks for waking me up," Shadow snarled angrily. Ever since he was acting nice when he took us in, he'd been rude and grumpy, and I didn't know why. "See you later," he said, and just as he was about to fly out of the hole, he realized that it was only sundown and the moon hadn't come out yet. He turned to glare at us. "And early, too!" he shrieked, his red pupils dilating.

Suddenly, said Browntuft, in a weak voice, "Shadow, I caught a mouse for you."

The Eagle Owl turned to look at him, and his eyes widened when he saw the small mouse. "Hmm. Not bad, I suppose." He gobbled it down, not even leaving the bones. Then he peeked out of the hole. Shadow's temper seemed to have lowered, because he looked at me. "I'm sorry. I was merely hungry. You two can eat the cloud rats; that's my apology," he said. Here was the Shadow we had met before! His voice became soft and silky again.

I looked at him to say that it was okay, but he had already flown into the night.

CHAPTER 6

FIRST RAIN

Ipeered out of the hollow, and right away, I noticed something. It was thunderstorming and the scent of rain clogged my nostrils.

When most eaglets thought of lightning, they thought of jagged cracks across the sky. That was not lightning. The sky, not just a crack, seemed to flash like the Ibon Spirit was taking revenge on the planet. It almost blinded me, and a spray of hard rain hit me in the face as I tried to turn away. Thunder boomed almost instantaneously after the sky turned silver.

The last storm was almost …right before my Choosing. Now, this one marked the start of the new rainy season. It had been six moons since I last saw my family. Six moons since we had last been together.

My sister…my mother…my father…what were they doing now? Were they coping without me? I felt a sudden aching desire to see them again, to feel my sister's warm wings as she covered me from the pit-patter of the rain, getting soaked for me. My mother's kind words as she brushed tails with me and consoled me, muttering that it would be fine, and it would clear up soon. My father teasingly saying that he would stand guard against the rain, he would fight it, and he wouldn't let it get to me.

What I wouldn't give to see them again!

Escape, escape, escape. The word throbbed in my head.

I tried to ignore the feelings of longing as Browntuft and I ate a squirrel that Shadow had caught, and right now the Owl was passed out on his bed, since he had hunted a lot last night. I glanced outside again, and the rain was already starting to pass, the clouds shifting to reveal the sunlight. After I finished swallowing a bone, the only sign that it had rained was the flooding ground and dripping leaves. Even the leafy floor of the hollow had somehow managed to get wet.

I shoved the scraps of the squirrel out of the hollow. "Browntuft, it's time to go hunting." It was like something that I did without thinking now. Browntuft walked toward the edge of the hole, and we both launched ourselves off the edge of the tree and started flying around. I flapped my wings, feeling the feathers on my back rearrange. I flapped again, but more on one side so I would turn to look at Browntuft. *Escape, escape, escape.*

I flew in the trees, from soaking perch to soaking perch, while Browntuft circled above. In this way, we managed to always catch at least two animals. I liked eating squirrels. I never had before, but my time with Shadow had shown me that squirrels made a really succulent treat. We hunted one squirrel, one vole, and a palm civet. Browntuft was so excited when I caught the civet. I remembered when I first met him, and he had loved eating the civet, even though he hadn't tasted it before.

"I want to eat this when we get back to the hole," he said. "Shadow is going to face me if he doesn't let me."

I had a feeling that he wanted the palm civet to himself, so I gently hinted, "Yeah—I'll love to share it." Maybe Browntuft got my tone, because the glint in his eyes faded a little. But he probably thought that even half a civet was better than none at all.

When we came in, it was already moonrise.

Shadow was awake, and he blinked at us as he entered. "Eat the civet." With that, he flew out. Now it was his turn to hunt for morning mealtime.

This had become how we lived. Shadow rarely exchanged conversation with us. Sometimes he would say "yes" or "no" or "eat this," but other than that, almost no complete sentences. Maybe he just wanted peace and quiet.

I was tired from carrying the heavy civet. Browntuft and I quickly preened, ate the civet, savoring the juicy, warm flesh, and then leaned against the burnt walls of the hollow and allowed sleep to overcome us.

Browntuft and I woke up to a loud crash, but there was no light shining from outside of the hole. I wondered what had woken me up, and Browntuft too, when I noticed the large brown figure on the floor in front of us. I slowly stalked forward, Browntuft following me. I prodded the figure, and turned it over. Then I gasped.

It was Shadow. And he had been attacked.

§   §   §

Even though Shadow had trapped us and forced us here, I still felt a sense of belonging—owing, even—to him, for possibly saving our lives. And I was pretty sure he had. I had heard from my Aerie before I was cast out that there was Human activity in the area.

Browntuft probably felt belonging, too, because he let out a little squeal of horror. I wanted to panic. But it wouldn't help him in this state.

Shadow had something embedded in his stomach that looked like a thorn, only it was gray and looked Human-made. The cut was not long or deep. The thorn was clotting up the blood. I didn't want to pull it out, but I held my talons over the thorn. Then the Eagle Owl stirred and looked up at us in confusion for a moment. This was bad. Really bad. Confusion wasn't on Shadow's list of faces, which included dark, mysterious, brooding, and, of course, unreadable—his favorite. Confusion was so obscure that I could hardly recognize it. There must have been something in the thorn to induce this confusion.

"Browntuft," I muttered. "Get some young leaves, and get them *quick.*"

Browntuft hurried out, and returned carrying a few leaves. I took a deep breath then yanked out the thorn. I plastered the fresh leaves onto Shadow's wounds. It was the best I could do to keep the wound from getting dirty. I wished I had been a healer. Darktail, my mother, would easily have patched up the Eagle Owl's wounds and used some kind of herb on it.

I looked at Browntuft. His amber eyes showed worry and fear that Shadow would die. So did I, even though that worry was mixed with a sense of reproach. Why were we taking care of Shadow? A voice in my head answered, *Because he took you in*. And why did he take us in? Well, that was one of life's mysteries.

"I guess we can only hope for the best," I said. I felt my heart beat fast. I opened the Eagle Owl's wings to see if there were wounds there, but there were none. Shadow stirred underneath me. He looked around; saw the thorn lying several talon-lengths away. Then his head dropped again.

For a moment, I felt like when Scarletcrest had fallen off the platform during training. I opened my beak to scream before I heard the steady *thumps* of Shadow's heart, and sighed with relief. I walked back over to the wall, and leaned against it. I could only leave this to the Ibon Spirit. I fell asleep watching the chest of the prone figure rapidly rise and fall.

Escape, escape, escape.

§   §   §

When I woke up, it was morning, and the sun's light streamed into the hollow. I remembered last night's catastrophe, and looked at Shadow. Of course, he was still sleeping, but I slowly crept towards him and lifted him up a little to check on his wound. The wound had scabbed over. Hopefully, this would prevent it from getting infected. I leaned back and stared at him. A few days ago, he seemed so strong, so mysterious. Now so weak, so dependent. If it weren't for us, he would probably die.

"Looks like you did a good job." I started in surprise, then realized that it was only Browntuft. I turned around and saw the young Hawk-Eagle approaching.

"You almost scared the life out of me," I said. "Well, my mother would have done better, but this might work for now."

"Your mother?" Browntuft's eyes showed inquisitiveness. "My parents died when I was only a moon old."

"I'm sorry to hear that," I said.

"Well, I guess we should go hunting?" he asked. I welcomed the suggestion. Anything, *anything,* to take my mind off Browntuft's tragic past.

"Sure, whatever you want," I said.

Browntuft lowered his crest. "Well, if you don't want to—"

"I do," I interrupted, then flew out of the hole, not waiting for him. The forest was cold and unforgiving. Mist blanketed the forest, like it was matching the mood. I dove through the layer of mist, feeling the droplets of water prickling on the bare skin near my beak.

Last night's events must have shaken me. I missed a civet that looked like it would have been nice eating if I had caught it, but managed to get a small squirrel and a medium-sized cloud rat. Browntuft managed to catch a water vole and a small bird. As we hunted, Browntuft stopped looking somber and started cheering up, enough that he actually started to joke about Shadow's wounds.

As we entered through the entrance, a low voice rasped, "Well, I guess I'm the subject of a joke now."

I didn't have time to look before there was a *whoosh* of wings and I glimpsed a dark shape flying out of the hollow.

I'd never seen Shadow hunt before, but now I watched in amazement as he dipped underneath the treeline and emerged carrying a mouse in his talons. And even though he was hurt! He had healed far faster than I had expected. I continued watching until I started to grow tired, and walked over to the wall where Browntuft was already waiting. Maybe I had been wrong about this being the last day. Shadow's wounds had given me a change of mind. I would have to escape one way or another, be it a moon from now or tomorrow. Without a word, I sank into a restless slumber.

CHAPTER 7

A PLAN

I woke up to the chirps of the morning birds and walked over to the food supply hole. It was bursting. The bark cover was breaking in the middle, and I quickly removed it before it broke. The hole was stuffed with all kinds of mice.

I heard a *screech*. Shadow flew in, panting, carrying a mouse. "Well? What are you doing?" he snapped. "Get hunting! I'm not late..." he glanced out of the hollow " ... or am I ..." Suddenly, he doubled over choking, looking just like when he was sleeping, except this time he was awake.

"*Screech, screech,* what are you doing? I—*screech, screech,* go to sleep—!" He screamed in pain, and fell over.

I froze. My throat felt clogged up. Tentatively, I moved forward and touched the Eagle Owl's chest. It was moving, but just barely. Just barely. Shadow was *just barely* holding on to life. Despite Browntuft's comments yesterday, he had given a cry of horror when Shadow fell over, and now was rushing at him, checking his heartbeat, preening his feathers, smoothing out his wings.

I looked him over, but saw nothing to suggest a head wound. I took off the leaves that covered his wound. I had never put leaves on the wounds again! Who had put them on? I inhaled sharply when I saw what was underneath.

It was another dart, sunk deep into his stomach, like the Humans who had done this had come back for another go. I yanked it out. It was tipped with a dark substance.

"Is it bad?" asked Browntuft.

"Come here and look for yourself."

Browntuft stalked closer, and bent his head to see what lay under the leaves. I realized, with a start, that Shadow had probably put them on when the dart had entered his body.

"Great Ibon Spirit!" Browntuft screeched in shock when he saw the pus. "Is he going to heal?"

"He will," I said. "But we need help."

"What?" Browntuft asked. "How?"

"We're going to get my mother. She's a Healer."

"Okay...But when?"

I twisted my beak, estimating. "Tomorrow, at dawn."

§ § §

I watched Shadow stir and look up. "What?" he asked, his voice heavy with sleep. He sank back into his slumber. At dusk, we had filled up the food hole with mice and squirrels so he wouldn't starve when we left.

"Well?" Browntuft asked beside me. "Do you agree that he won't wake up again? Then we can go get help?" His eyes glinted in the shadow of the curved wall in the corner of the hollow. Of course, we weren't *escaping*, but Shadow might not let us go out from the hollow, even for his own health.

"Not yet," I rasped. "Wait for it..." Shadow thrashed once, and then went still again. "Now!" We had been planning this for the rest of the night after Shadow had come back. First, we waited until he thrashed. Once he did, it would be a while before he woke up again, and this would give us enough time to fly out, get our bearings in the dark, and then fly to the Aerie. It was simple enough.

What if my Aerie tried to kill me? Well, I had an entire speech planned out, where I said, "Keeneye's word dies with her," even though that was cruel. But I had a feeling with all this happening, I wouldn't be killed. Nothing could stop me now.

I slowly walked across the hollow towards the opening, careful to tread quietly. Earlier this day, Browntuft and I had swept a path on the wooden floor so that the leaves wouldn't crunch under our talons. Shadow lay there, still, smaller now that he wasn't awake. Glimmers of morning light came into the hollow, and I carefully stayed in the shadows, picking my way towards the entrance. Shadow was motionless.

I was almost at the opening—one third of a wing away—when suddenly Shadow convulsed on the floor.

He opened wide eyes and started screaming angrily, "No! No! I won't!" But then he sighed and collapsed into sleep again. I watched in horror. Every time he convulsed, it would be soon before he opened his eyes and started acting what we called "the Awake Phase," meaning he was aware of everything and acted normal for ten minutes. I had to hurry. I increased my speed, but as I walked near Shadow, who slept near the entrance, something happened.

Maybe I cawed and I didn't realize it, or maybe my tail brushed him, but either way, he opened his eyes.

"Now, where are you going?" he asked smoothly. He stalked towards me and Browntuft. His moment of respite had passed, and now he was back in his crazy phase.

Browntuft launched himself into the dawn sky. I followed him, and looked back at the Eagle Owl to see if he would be following us.

"You can't go!" he screamed. "The Humans are—" He stopped and grimaced. Shadow only convulsed on the floor again as we flew into the early morning, the sun just touching the treetops.

CHAPTER 8

RETURN

We set off at a quick pace—east, towards my Aerie. I could hardly see, the leaves were just green blurs against brown markings, and when we flew across the narrow sea, the normally crystalline waters seemed a murky shade of gray.

As we went, we didn't talk, but this allowed me to think over the fact that we left Shadow alone, in his crazy state. What would happen to him? And what did he mean about the Humans? There was no way that the Humans would even come this far into the rainforest. As we flew, my mind started to calm down. I was pretty sure that he was delusional.

I inspected a tree, and couldn't hold back a squeal of excitement when I saw the horizontal cross with a diagonal line.

"Look," I announced. "We are officially near my Aerie!"

I whined to myself quietly, "Almost there... almost there ..." until we reached a tree that had a horizontal cross. My frantic eyes probed the bark, searching for the deciding factor of the diagonal slash under, but there was none. I couldn't stop yelping in excitement when I looked ahead and saw a familiar tree with one branch oddly bent. We had called it Bent-branch tree when I was still in the Aerie.

We were near the Aerie! So close, but I still wasn't sure whether or not they would capture me or try to kill me. I increased speed, forgetting Browntuft until he rasped behind me.

"Wait up."

Even then, I only slowed my speed a little, but stopped when I heard a telltale screeching.

I looked up at the sun. Yes, it was noon. When the sun had reached the highest, the Territorial Flocks would already be sent out ... *Oh no*, I thought. *If they were to find me, I would surely be captured, even if I wasn't an outcast.* The crime of being with another bird was crime enough.

I took a break on a tree to prepare myself, and Browntuft followed suit.

"Where is it?" a voice rasped from the direction of the patrol. I started in shock, barely hiding my shriek of astonishment.

It was my sister, Lightfeather.

§　　§　　§

I bit down, forcing my beak to stay shut, but inside, screeches were piercing my head. Browntuft saw the look cross my face. He glanced curiously at me.

"Who was that?" he asked quietly. "Your mother?"

I shook my head frantically and twitched my beak to tell him to stay quiet. He got the message, and stopped talking.

"My sister," I rasped slowly.

Even though Browntuft didn't know her, he squealed quietly in surprise, but stopped the high-pitched sound quickly.

"What's her name?" he asked curiously.

I twitched my beak in exasperation. Just then, a few leaves were dislodged from the tree next to us, and an entire Territorial Flock of Philippine Eagles flew out onto the tree I was on.

Browntuft flew to another perch behind the tree. His dark brown plumage blended him into the bark. I soared into the tree's top, aiming to hide in the leaves, and I flew into them just in time before a bird—my sister—thought to look up at me.

Maybe I dislodged a few leaves, because my sister opened her beak in surprise, looking straight at me. "I'll scout in this area, and you can head north. Go on now," Lightfeather said.

The birds exchanged a few glances. I started in shock when I saw another Eagle sidle closer to Lightfeather, whose crest went up. I recognized the signs. Lightfeather liked this bird.

I searched my mind for the name, but it evaded me. "Lightfeather, I should guard your back," he said.

My sister let out a little screech of delight. "The flock will be waiting for you. You'd better go," she warned.

The Eagle looked unsure of himself.

"You know," she said. "If you want that egg..."

That seemed to persuade him. He gave a last rueful look at Lightfeather, then flew away. What was that about an *egg*? As far as I knew, Lightfeather had never been interested in being a mother, which led me to believe that this was some sort of make-believe of theirs. I almost smiled.

Lightfeather looked up at my hiding place. She cawed up, "I know you're there. Even though I don't know who, I feel like I know you."

I shivered, despite the warm and humid weather. Slowly, I walked out of the leaves on the branch I was on.

Lightfeather stared at me for a moment in surprise. Then she flew up to me, shrieking in delight.

"Great Ibon Spirit! Brazenclaw told me you were dead, but I never believed it! We never found your body....Swiftwing!" Sadness suddenly overcame her features. "Come back to the Aerie."

I shook my head, surprised that she would say such a thing. "Really?" I asked skeptically. "Um, they'll kill me? Lightfeather?"

"Not if you're under my protection," she said slowly and hesitantly. "If you come, I can guarantee that you'll survive. I can't guarantee your freedom, though..." She brushed her wings against mine, and then jerked her head in the direction of the Aerie. "By the way, I think you have somebird with you."

"No, I don't," I said, feeling horrible that I was lying to my nestmate. "You probably—no, you did—think wrong."

"No!" Lightfeather screeched. "Since when have you lied to me? Are you full-grown now? I *know* I saw a flash of brown, and I know that it's probably another species, but it's fine since I won't be angry. Really."

"You sure?" I asked doubtfully. It was hard to believe that she wouldn't crest-up if I showed her Browntuft. Finally, I nodded. "Promise."

"I promise."

"Browntuft, come out!" I shrieked quietly. "I promise that you won't get captured, like, really!"

There was a rustle of branches and leaves, and a few fell down from where the Hawk-Eagle was standing. After a few brown movements in which I saw his amber eyes, he stepped clear of the tree trunk and was face-to-face with Lightfeather.

First, Lightfeather opened her beak to scream. Second, I brushed her with my wing and, remembering herself, she closed it, looking embarrassed. "Well, I made a mess of my promise, didn't I," she said, looking down at her talons. "That's a good disguise. Did you use mud and leaves? But how did you get that small size and the eyes? He's absolutely puny!"

"That's not a joke!" I said vehemently. "That's *actually* a Philippine Hawk-Eagle!"

"Well, if you say so," Lightfeather said doubtfully. She slowly walked the length of the branch to Browntuft, held up a talon, and poked him. He couldn't hold back a squeal of protest, and I watched, half amused, half horrified, as Lightfeather let a little shriek of horror and flew away from him in a flurry of feathers. "You're right," she gasped. "That's genuine." I remembered the ridiculous way I had felt when I had seen Browntuft—malice in eyes, wicked talons—and I could imagine what Lightfeather was feeling like. I watched my sister and my best friend meet each other. After a long moment of silence, I changed the subject.

"Well, can you take me back to the Aerie? I need to get help from our mother and it can't wait." I asked.

Lightfeather half opened her beak at me in astonishment. "Really?" she asked quietly, her voice almost a rasp. "Father doesn't really take well to having a different species in his Aerie. You know, since he sort of hates other species of birds."

I looked into her eyes carefully, making sure she understood my next word. "Yes."

For a moment, we stared at each other, a triangle of gazes.

Then Browntuft broke the silence by saying, "Can I come?"

I couldn't believe my ears. I whirled around, moving my gaze from Lightfeather's to his.

"Um..." I started. He cut me off, putting his talon forward on my chest. Then he opened his beak to speak.

"Let's go." With that, he started flying south, coincidentally in the direction of the Aerie.

The flight was fast. In no time, we were back in that little clearing in the forest, and Browntuft was barely lagging. We had to rest one or two times, but other than that, we had almost no pauses. I couldn't hold back a screech of excitement and happiness as I saw my father and mother on one of the platforms in the trees. Another one held Sharpbeak, Tawnytop and Scarletcrest. *So Scarletcrest is their mother,* I thought.

Suddenly, as if she had sensed me, I could see Scarletcrest's oddly colored crest angle as it moved to view me. I watched in horror as she jumped off the platform and flew to me, talons aimed at my face, shrieking, "Outcast!" in a screech that shattered the stillness of the rainforest.

CHAPTER 9

RETRIEVAL

"Continue the story," said Father. His dark blue eyes never left my face.

Almost instinctively, I looked to Browntuft to answer, only to remember he had been escorted away. "You were the only ones who could help us, since Browntuft's Aerie would probably kill us like they had intended to do to Browntuft in the form of sending him away. Mother, Darktail, could probably heal Shadow," I replied.

We were on the Leader's platform, talking to my father, who had turned out to be the new Leader. Apparently, after Keeneye's death, they had held the Leader's Selection, and Fierceheart, my father, had won by a near hundred votes.

After Scarletcrest had charged me, Lightfeather had knocked her away and taken me to see Father. Having to use my speech, I convinced him to "hear me out," mainly because I told them that there was an Eagle Owl in the area who knew something about Humans.

"—and so, we found Lightfeather, and she led us here," I finished. The birds, Father's inner circle, were quiet. Scarletcrest was part of the inner circle now. Then there was Sharpbeak, who was an Eaglet Advisor, an Advisor-in-training and who couldn't vote, Lightfeather's mate, Lightfeather, and two more I didn't know.

"Silverneck, yes?" Father asked, addressing one of the Eagles I didn't know.

"She has the hint of truth," said the Philippine Eagle called Silverneck, turning out to be female. Her screech wasn't guttural, but smooth and melodious. "I can see it. I say that she should be welcome, and *unharmed.*"

The other unknown, who was actually Father's enemy, snarled, "So! Just 'cause she's Leader's Daughter she's innocent? I say sentence her to death, following Keeneye's original order!"

"Quiet." My father's voice was a harsh and cold rasp. "Restrain yourself, Highhead. I will not accept outbursts in my inner circle."

"Well then I'll!" said Scarletcrest angrily. Her crest flared up in emotion. "I say sentence her to death, and I agree with Highhead, my mate. You've no right to insult him."

Huh. So Highhead was her mate, and also Sharpbeak and Tawnytop's father. Made sense. Like Eagle, like Eaglet.

"I think that she is telling the truth," Lightfeather said, darting a triumphant glance in the direction of Scarletcrest, Sharpbeak and Highhead. "She's innocent, definitely. I agree with Grayspan."

So that was the name of the bird that she liked!

"That leaves my choice," said Father. "It is clear as water that my daughter is telling the truth. She is innocent. Yes, Swiftwing?"

"Father," I rasped. "We should go to Shadow. He's wise and strong, and I think that you should heal him. He got really hurt and I think that you could help him."

For a moment, there was silence. Then, "What do you take us for, nutbrains?" It was Highhead. "We know never to help any Owls, much less *Eagle* Owls. If we did, could I be the one to interrogate him?" His crest bristled in excitement. "I have ways, you know, of getting information. He won't resist."

"Who said anything about interrogating him?!" I cried. "No, you're thinking along the wrong lines. He's a good bird. He wasn't hiding anything! He just took us in!"

"Aim for the eyes," said Highhead dreamily. "Claw them out and the target won't ever stand a chance."

"Ugh!" I recoiled from him in disgust. That was just gruesome. I hoped that Highhead hadn't done that before. If he had, I found it hard to believe that it was allowed. Maybe he had done it in secret...

"Yes," Highhead snapped back, the dreamy quality no longer in his eyes. It was replaced by maliciousness. "Owls, even if they're wise, are always evil, my young, innocent Eaglet. In no way should you trust them. *They always have a second reason.*"

"Fine," I said. "Let's go. But no torture!"

"No torture," Father agreed.

§ § §

We set out at once. It was morning and so we first hunted and ate. Then we started flying north again. It was actually not supposed to be public, so the flock consisted of only a few that didn't need to be in the Aerie at that particular moment: Highhead, Sharpbeak, Lightfeather,

Silverneck, and another Philippine Eagle called Longtalon. And, of course, me. Father couldn't come because his absence would be noticed, but Mother came, since she was a Healer. And Browntuft was still being "momentarily detained."

The forest was cool in the early morning. I could imagine that we were just a normal hunting flock, and not a specialized one set aside to retrieve Shadow.

"Formation!" Highhead screeched. Unfortunately, he had been appointed as the Head of the Tracking Flock, and so he was allowed to give orders. Highhead, Sharpbeak, Lightfeather, and Silverneck all moved into a pattern, with Highhead in front, Sharpbeak and Lightfeather next to each other behind him, and Silverneck and Longtalon behind them. Darktail lingered at the back, flying near the flock but not in the formation. Her talons were heavy with a bundle of fragrant leaves.

I looked around in confusion. Where was I supposed to go? Highhead seemed to realize his mistake, and I had a feeling that it had been on purpose. "Oh, what about you? I seemed to have missed you. Usually, it's only five Warriors, but since you're Leader's Daughter, we have to include a Hunter. You don't seem to know about Formation." He turned away from me in contempt. "Well, we'll have to stretch the rules to allow you to fit." Suddenly, he turned around and faced the others. "Silverneck and Longtalon! What are you doing, you lazywings? Move forward. You, my innocent Eaglet, behind both of them in the middle. You'll have to be by yourself."

Silverneck glared at me. Whatever had prompted her to take my side during the vote had gone now. In fact, she wasn't as kind as I had thought.

Silverneck gave me a dirty look. "Thanks!" She hissed underneath her breath. "Now Highhead said I was a lazywings! Never. In. My. Life!" She turned away from me just as the Tracking Flock started to move forward. The leaves moved faster. Mist had started to settle, so it was getting harder to see.

Calling out directions, soon we were at Shadow's Hollow.

The burned, huge hole in the tree was visible, almost like a beacon in the afternoon.

Highhead beckoned me forward, moving his wing in one sweeping gesture towards the hole. I flew to the head of the Flock, until I was at the mouth of the hole. I landed on one of the nearby boughs.

§ § §

Shadow was sleeping. He was lying facedown on his bed of dead leaves, and he was gently moving. I slowly stalked towards him, but he didn't move. Just a dark brown shape who seemed so weak, so vulnerable in this form.

Encouraged, I went faster. As I neared him, one of my talons went out and flipped him over. The blood from the dart wound had been replaced with pus.

Darktail gasped as she saw the wound.

"Let me help—" she started, but I cut her off with a curt flare of my crest. She turned to me, and I could see a Healer's determination in her eyes. Ignoring me, she walked to the Eagle Owl and started to fix him up. By the time Darktail was done mending him, the flock had set up something that looked like a nest with vines sticking out of each of the four corners. I grabbed Shadow by the shoulders and laid him on the nest. Highhead stood forward and secured Shadow with vines, looping the plant around his body.

Each female took a vine and started to fly. It was laborious, but soon we started to get the rhythm and hang of it.

CHAPTER 10

TRIAL

We held Shadow's trial an hour after his retrieval, when we decided that he was innocent or that he deserved to be interrogated. My mother had dressed and covered his wounds, and by the time I saw him, looking ever so proud, it was hard to believe that he had ever been crazy from his wounds.

"Some type of poison on the dart," Mother had fretted, looking everywhere in her Healer stores. "The herb, Feather-tail, that heals it, only grows in the Year of the Hawk-Eagle, and the Year of the Western Osprey,

last year, and right now it's our year. Fortunately, I collected some during

the Western Osprey year, and since it's only been a year it shouldn't be too

weak." Mother had taken out a leaf that had bristles on the end, and had

crushed it in her talons. The juice had streamed out, and with expert little

dabs, she had applied the liquid to Shadow's wounds. Then my mother

covered it with fresh leaves.

Now, I held back a little pant of astonishment as I saw Shadow

stride in. Two other Philippine Eagles were next to him, Warriors by the

look of it, and towered over him. But with the aura of pride and confidence

Shadow gave off, they might as well have been minuscule, or not even there.

The Warriors had seemed to realize it, and their faces were pure spite and

anger. They looked excited, as if they were happy that Shadow would be

tried. I, for myself, felt horrified. Now that Shadow was awake, I didn't feel

quite as bold, but I was ready to speak my mind against any accusations.

"Presenting: Shadow Leanmouth, the Eagle Owl!" said Father,

residing at the front of the platform.

Um, who was Leanmouth? I was tempted to ask that before

Longtalon, the bird who was next to me on the Leader's Platform,

whispered, "That's his secret name. All Eagle Owls have a second name and

when they're questioned they use it. But their name can never be found out, so they usually just make up one, otherwise it's embarrassing."

Highhead said, "Swiftwing, state the wrongs that Shadow Leanmouth did." His voice trembled with happiness, here in his own element of trial.

I turned to look at him, and he moved back, signaling that I should go to the middle of the platform. So I stalked forward, my legs straight. Shadow watched me with almost detached amusement, like he couldn't believe I was following the proceedings correctly.

"No wrongs," I said clearly, since Shadow hadn't done any. I couldn't believe that I had said that, when before, I would have just nodded timidly.

It was a good thing that it was only Father, Mother, Scarletcrest, Sharpbeak and the Tracking Flock on the platform and that it was quite large, or else Highhead would have probably knocked them over with his wings. Shadow blinked his yellow eyes at me, and I knew that he was surprised, even though he didn't show it. Father conveyed his subtle anger by raising his crest.

"What are you doing?" Highhead hissed. "Say, 'His wrongs: Capturing the Hawk-Eagle and me, starving the Hawk-Eagle and me, and wounding the Hawk-Eagle and me.'"

"Okay, number one, his name's not just the Hawk-Eagle! It's

Browntuft, and you know it, Highhead! Two, Shadow hasn't done any of that!" The Philippine Eagle glared at me until I found myself looking down at the floor.

"Is there anyone who would like to defend Shadow?" asked Highhead. When no one raised their crest in answer, he nodded. Since I had been forced to accuse him and Browntuft wasn't here, still being questioned, I couldn't defend him either.

"My Leader, do you pronounce the interrogation official? Will he be exposed to all the ways of taking information?" Highhead asked. His head was high, just like his name, and he was gazing proudly up at Father. He added, under his breath, "Fierceheart, say yes. I promised, no torture, but there's something else I can do…" His eyes twinkled, and Scarletcrest let out a little rasp of excitement. Obviously, she was also excited to extract information from him.

"No torturing, but let's find out what he knows about the Humans!" said Father impatiently. He dipped his head formally at Highhead and looked away.

"Yes, thank you, my Leader. When shall I start?"

"In sixty heartbeats time," said Father.

"Well," Highhead and Scarletcrest both said, looking at each other, their crests halfway up in the air. "Then let's get started. Let Shadow

Leanmouth's interrogation begin!"

CHAPTER II

INTERROGATION

Shadow held his head high, turning away from Highhead almost contemptuously.

"I have a question," said Highhead through a gritted beak, "why did you take the Hawk-Eagle and Swiftwing in?" After being cleverly deflected for a few rounds, he was at his patience's edge. "If you don't answer, I'll take out your feathers, one by one."

Shadow somehow looked imperiously down at him, even though he was shorter than Highhead. "I don't think so," he said smoothly. "If you did, I would be in too much pain to answer." He smiled. "Or, I might just kill myself. Maybe an *accidental* fall from a tree, and without feathers, I wouldn't be able to fly."

Highhead fluffed his crest up. "Answer me, Eagle Owl!" he screamed, and started to advance on Shadow, who only looked at him coolly. Then, suddenly, Shadow's red pupils started to dilate until they completely overwhelmed the yellow. I took in a deep breath, knowing something was about to happen. Even though Highhead hadn't lived with him, he backed away too.

Shadow keeled over and started to shriek, writhing on the ground like a snake. Highhead lost his composure and gasped and flew to the other side of the platform.

"I swear that I can pluck out your feathers!" he shouted, holding out one talon to him. "Answer me! Why did you take them in?" Shadow looked up at him. His pupils had gone a little smaller, but it was only a thin sliver of yellow that we could see.

"Great Ibon Spirit!" Shadow cackled, getting up and flapping his wings everywhere. "Save them, now! Save them! It's Humans!" He screeched once and collapsed, still writhing. I jerked away from him in horror. He finally said, "Move! Move south! Now! Or else!" He fell silent.

Highhead regained his composure and rushed forward to check

on his heartbeat. I did the same. It was still steady, but every ten counts it would go really fast for two heartbeats and then go back to normal.

"Get a Healer," Highhead rasped, his pale eyes pointed at me. *Oh no. What was going to happen to Shadow? Would he die?* Without another thought, I jumped off the platform and flew to my family's platform.

Once there, I panted, "Mother, bring the Feather-tail herb! Shadow is going crazy again!"

"No," said Mother. "That's the wrong herb. Leaf-wing is the correct one." She took a pair of large leaves and took off after me.

As we arrived, Mother didn't even stop to gasp, which was surprising, this being the first time she had seen Shadow crazy. Instead, without a word, she crushed the Leaf-wing in her talons and then trickled the green juices into Shadow's open beak.

He stopped convulsing and screaming, just saying, "Save and move, save and move!"

Finally, he fell asleep. His chest rose and fell slowly, and Highhead gritted his beak. It was obvious that he had wished to get more information out of him. What had that been about moving and saving us?

"Well," Highhead snarled, "We'll have to continue tomorrow, I guess. Slash it!" he cursed angrily. He stalked to the edge of the platform and flew away. Slowly, I crept towards Shadow and prodded him in the chest. His heartbeat was strong and steady. The odd fast heartbeats had gone away. I backed away from him, just in case he lashed out.

Suddenly, in a flurry of wings, a Philippine Eagle—Longtalon—flew toward Shadow, onto the platform. Regardless of his rank, I shoved him aside and leapt protectively over Shadow, my legs splayed over him.

Longtalon circled for a moment then alighted slowly next to me. "What was that for?" he asked, sounding wounded. "I was just going to look at him." His eyes glinted mischievously. "Or not. Fine, you got me. Highhead's orders." In a monotonic caw, he added, "Please move out of the way, Leader's daughter. I have come to pick up Shadow Leanmouth."

I moved aside and let him through.

"Well, I've got to go. Highhead'll be waiting for me," he said. With a last flick of his tail, he signaled three helpers and they all flew off, carrying Shadow on a contraption like when we had retrieved him.

§　　§　　§

I sighed and shook my wings out, rearranging the pinions. I jumped off the platform. A short flight would cool my head off. As I glided, I shook my crest out, feeling the cold air rushing through.

I was making good progress, almost a full circle of the clearing in the forest, when suddenly there were a few squawks in front of me, and I flew haltingly forward, knowing something was wrong. How? Because Father was there, and he was Leader, only coming to important events. And there was also Longtalon. It worried me, because Longtalon was looking completely crest-up. It was obvious something had happened, but what? Longtalon was always calm and composed like my father. But he'd regained composure quickly, and right now, by the looks of it, terror had been on his beak for a long time. The tranquility of the forest disappeared, noises becoming louder and more garish, suddenly. Things in the background blurred out.

"Swiftwing!" Father panted when he saw me. It was obvious that he had been frantic, because his feathers were astray, and a few were stuck to his talons. This worried me more than Longtalon. Two always calm, composed Eagles, completely mad with something.

"What?" I asked, trying to sound innocent, just in case I was in trouble or something. Father opened his beak to speak, but Longtalon beat him to it. He muttered something to me, and I craned my neck closer to hear him. "What?" I repeated again, starting to really get interested.

"Humans are attacking the Aerie!" he repeated angrily. I sucked my breath in. Well, we could always move to another Aerie, couldn't we—But Longtalon hadn't finished his warning of doom. "And," he added, taking in a shaky breath, "They killed Shadow!"

CHAPTER 12

HUMAN

Shadow. Dead.

Oh my sky.

Shadow dying had never seemed to occur to me. First, Keeneye. Then Shadow. Who was next? Mother? Father? Browntuft? *What was happening?*

"I know," said Longtalon, sounding like he was faking being sad. "It's hard to take in. It almost killed me with shock when I heard about it."

"Yeah, I bet so!" I screamed at him. He backed away, his eyes round and hurt, but I hadn't finished. "You barely knew him! Yeah, you definitely felt sad for him! You didn't know him like I did. I..." My voice trailed away, and I buried my head in Father's chest. He wrapped his wings around me.

"Now, now," he said. I felt a wave of anger at him, Longtalon, the Humans and myself, because if I had been alert, I probably could have prevented this. Now Shadow was dead because of me! "It's sad," Father sympathized. I tore myself away from him, trying to avoid his eyes where I knew I would see the wounded look. I wasn't the eagletish, younger version of myself. And I needed to show that to Father.

"I need to think," I said.

Longtalon looked disappointed. "Of course." He let out a low caw. "Well, while you're thinking, we'll be busy *fighting Humans...*"

That shook me out of my stupor, and with a start, I realized that Humans were attacking the Aerie for real.

Without a word to either of the males, I jumped off the platform, ignoring the shouts behind me. I flapped my wings hard, wanting to get away from these uncaring Eagles. I flapped again, and again, forcing myself to fly faster. I closed my beak with a snap.

As I emerged from the ring of trees that surrounded the clearing, I gasped. True to Father's word, there were five Humans, all wearing dark green shirts and pants with light green mottled patterns on them, breaking up their appearance, so when they moved they almost disappeared.

Over their shoulder they carried what looked like long sticks, but these were thicker and were a dark, shiny gray, like when it rained and the tree bark grew all shiny. They started off thick but tapered off at the end, and were hollow, with an obvious hole at the narrow end.

The Human in front moved the rod forward on his shoulder, squinting one cruel brown eye and pointing the hole in the narrow side at a bird. I watched in horror as the Human pulled back on something that was attached to the long rod, and something dark flashed through the air. There was a puff of smoke and a most horrendous *BANG!* Suddenly, the bird that the Hunter had pointed at, whom I didn't know, let out a long, keening, screeching cry, and collapsed, falling to the rainforest floor, a large black pellet stuck in its chest.

"No!" I screamed, rushing forward, the shriek rising to my beak unbidden. I was about to fly to the Philippine Eagle when the Human who shot him rushed forward, shouting in a loud guttural voice. Though the words were obscure, the meaning was clear enough. *Victory.* The human picked the bird up, grabbing the tips of its wings in each hand. Then he spread his arms apart. The Eagle had been a female, so its wingspan was far larger than the Human's. The Human made a loud, choking sound, and I realized he was chuckling. The Human doubled over, laughing. He took his long rod and poked it into the Eagle's chest, and then snorted again. Finally, he stopped laughing.

I couldn't believe I had been dashing at the Humans. I held myself back, staring in disbelief at the limp Eagle.

Another Human said something to him. Even though I couldn't understand them, I could still hear what they were saying, and I heard the second Human call him "Claudio." The first Human replied, still giggling, calling his friend "Albert." I watched, horrified. Giggling! When they had killed one of my own!

I figured out the rest of the Humans' names. The two I didn't know were Hubert and Jago. I realized something about the Humans, and it was that they all had cruel lines on their faces, were lean and muscular, and had those horrible, silvery rods.

Jago was distinctly fatter than the rest; he had a lot of hair on his upper lip and chin, and he moved with a clumsiness that any bird would have scorned. But he was still a good marksman.

"Guns," a grim voice said next to me. I turned to see Browntuft. "Shadow told me about them once, when you weren't listening. They have pellets called 'bullets' inside of them, and they're sort of like talons, I guess. They pierce through whatever they hit. Lethal. The users are called Poachers."

"Hi, Browntuft. Jago, Claudio, Albert and Hubert, you know," I said, hating how tremulous my voice sounded.

"What?"

"They're their names," I clarified, feeling my crest rising. "The Humans. I heard their names, but that's it. Don't think I'm a know-it-all or something."

"I won't," said Browntuft, amusement in his caw. I smiled at him, and half expected him to screech and leap back. Instead, he only smiled back. "Funny names, huh?"

"Ugh!" I said. "Did you know they killed one of our own?"

"Oh, flying feathers, Swiftwing! I didn't mean that!" he said, but it was too late. With those words, *Funny names, huh?* I had realized that Browntuft was still juvenile and sort of—callous. I was about to fly away, in fact, I was teetering on the edge of the platform, when there were a few guttural shouts from the Poachers below.

Claudio, the first Human, took aim and fired.

The noise was horror. The sound split my head open, and I reeled, shocked. My vision was filled with smoke, and half blind, when the bullet hit the branch next to me, and I screeched and flew away.

Jago took out his gun, and shot again. The noise left me winded, reeling. I could hardly think and see, but instinct told me to fly away. I tried to dodge the bullet. A horrible, aching feeling, started to well up in my stomach. I had never really realized that I could actually die. Now, thinking about it, I started to faint.

But Jago had anticipated it. He had shot above me, so as I flew, the bullet grazed my wing, tearing through my soft feathers and flesh. I screamed in pain. It was so sudden, like fire, first nothing and then a pain that flared up and hurt like crazy. I screeched and shrieked some more, hopping around on the platform, almost manic with the pain.

Black crept on the edge of my vision, a monster wanting to claim me. I forced myself not to succumb to unconsciousness, but it was too late. The waves of darkness that threatened to take me finally crashed over my vision. The last thing I felt was the ground starting to tremble.

§ § §

I woke to hazy shapes moving over me. I caught a glimpse of a smaller brown one. Browntuft. I blinked, and my vision cleared. My head instinctively turned to look at my wing, and my heart lifted when I saw that leaves already sealed the wound. Then I moved my wing, and felt a jolt of pain.

"Don't move it," a voice advised, and I realized it was Mother. I shuddered, and slowly put my wing back down. I took stock of my surroundings.

I was on the family platform. A few birds, including Browntuft surrounded me, looking at me with huge, worried eyes. At Darktail's flick of her wing, they dispersed. But Mother stayed there. "I was so worried," she started. "As soon as Browntuft told me, we came to find you. There was a minor earthquake, and the Humans ran away, leaving you on the ground." Her eyes darted away from me, not looking me in the face.

"I'm fine," I said. "I'll heal." I made a dismissive gesture with my wounded wing, my left wing, and a bolt of pain shot through it to my shoulder. I tried not to show it, but Mother had seen me wince.

"Are you okay?" asked Mother. "Really, you should rest." She rushed forward, pressing down on my shoulders to keep me on the bed of fresh leaves I was on. I turned my head, wondering what platforms I could see.

I saw Sharpbeak's family's platform. Tawnytop was ogling me, and even from here, I could see the spiteful glint in his pale gray-blue eyes. My gaze traveled to the one on top of it. My heart leapt.

It was the platform where Shadow had been killed. I saw his body, still there, with a large black bullet stuck in his chest. At least it had killed him, not put him in the intense pain that I was feeling right now. I felt a sudden jolt of anger that his body was still there.

"Why is he still there?" I asked.

"Who?" asked Mother. She looked up from a stack of dried Feather-tail herb that she had been sorting out. She threw a bundle of leaves so dry that they looked like husks over the edge of the platform. "Oh, Shadow?" she said, sounding relieved. "He's nothing. They'll throw him in a river or something."

"What?" I asked, astonished. "He warned you! He warned you about Humans and you go repaying him by *planning to throw him in a river?* Would you do it to me if I died?" The tradition for birds that died was that you threw them onto the ground from high up in a tree. And now this Aerie—my Aerie—was condemning this Eagle Owl that had taken me in, to a doomed life in the Ibon afterlife.

"I'm sorry!" said Mother, looking scared. She backed away from me on the confined space of the platform. "If you want, we can thrown him from a tree."

I nodded, and she sighed and relaxed.

"You're not angry at me?"

"Not if it wasn't your idea," I said. I felt pain suddenly coming from where the bullet had pierced my wing. Not like a sharp, stabbing pain, but more like a dull ache that threatened to overcome me. "Am I going to die?" I asked softly.

"Not if I can help it," replied Darktail.

"I think I'm going to black out," I murmured.

Mother dipped her head. "Okay. Rest. It'll be good for you." Satisfied that I had my mother, a Healer's word, I closed my eyes and sank back into a deep slumber.

CHAPTER 13

CAPTURE

I woke up. I was on a different platform, I could feel the different texture, the stone sticking into my back. I turned my head, blinking my eyes at the same time. This time, there was no bed of young leaves. I was lying straight on reddish-brown bark. I moved on the nest, trying to move the stone. Finally, it rolled over and I felt I could lie down peacefully.

Then I realized: Highhead stood in front of me, his beak twisted in a triumphant grin. "Interrogation," he said. His talons were tapping the red floor impatiently.

"No," I said blearily. "Shadow is dead. You can't interrogate him." I wondered for a moment why there were no leaves. Maybe they had healed my wing? My head angled to look at it. It was still patched up.

My question was answered when the horrible truth came to me. Shadow was dead, but Browntuft and I were still alive, and were a valuable source of good information. But what about Browntuft? Highhead answered my question as if he had read my mind. "The Hawk-Eagle is not one of our own, Leader's daughter. I am not even sure if you are."

My feathers bristled. I felt my crest rise up higher than it ever had. I pushed myself into a standing position, using my good wing. I yelped as my wounded wing gave a bolt of pain.

Highhead put his talon on my wound. "Now, this can be easy, or this can be hard," he crooned. "You can listen, or I can extend the length of your recovery."

He pressed down, and I screeched in pain as blood squirted out and splattered onto his and my feathers. "That was for silence," he said. "Be quiet, or else."

"Did Father even allow this?" I asked, knowing that his answer would be "Yes." Of course it would, otherwise that could be counted as treason, and he would be thrown out ...like me.

It surprised me when he shuffled his talons on the red-bark

platform. He looked at me, his pale eyes meeting my darker gaze. "What did I say?" he asked. "Silence." I knew what he meant, and I was surprised to find that I wasn't astonished. Highhead would do whatever he wanted to torture someone. Shadow had died too early, but I was still alive. I wanted to scream, I wanted to screech. But I kept silent and let the course of Highhead's torture continue.

§   §   §

Over the course of the afternoon, Highhead bit me twenty four times, scratched me seventeen times, and pushed on my bullet wound nineteen times. By the time he announced the interrogation "done," I was smarting all over, one wing almost numb with pain, the other with long scratches. My soft underbelly was covered in beak-bites, and my face was exploding with agony.

"Don't tell any bird," he warned as he flew off.

I watched his retreating tail. Then I collapsed. He had hit me so hard. I could see droplets of blood on the tree-nest where he had bit me, and my wing ... I chanced a look at it. It was worse than before. The ripped flesh was inflamed and red.

I took in a deep breath. When I had stepped up to the Leader's platform, I hadn't really expected to actually break tradition. Why me? I could have been like Sharpbeak, or Mother, just another normal Philippine Eagle in the Aerie. Why me? I hadn't done anything to deserve this. A normal bird wouldn't have been shot when they were barely three.

I have to hunt. The order rang around in my head, and I found myself leaning back, opening my wings. Then I felt a sudden blast of agony in my left wing. With a start, I remembered that I couldn't fly with this wound in my wing. Sighing, I settled down. I was stranded here.

Suddenly, there was a commotion at the edge of my platform. It was Highhead. He looked grim, not as snarky and regal as before. His crest was astray. He stared down at me, but his eyes conveyed his panic. "There's a female Human," he said, glaring at me as if this was my fault. "And it wants you." He raked the ground angrily, sending bark flying down. The hues of the forest suddenly became garish and bright. The leaves seemed to become thicker, pressing down on me.

"How do you know?" I asked, scratching my talons on the red-bark tree-nest.

Highhead glared right back at me. "I don't, you nutbrain! But it was pointing at you and there was also the one that shot you next to her. She kept on pointing at you and saying nonsense to the one that shot you."

"What?" I asked, confused. What would a Human want with me?

To eat me? That was disgusting. "What did it look like?"

"Female—didn't I tell you?" snapped Highhead. "And she wants you!"

"So?" I asked. Then I realized what he actually meant. She wants you—so what about you give her yourself? "Really?" I said. "You want me to give myself up for you?"

"Not for me," Highhead said, even though the look in his eyes said the opposite. "For the Aerie! I'm pretty sure the one who shot you will kill all of us if you don't." Even though Highhead did mean himself, I realized that what he had said was true. Jago, the Human, would probably kill us all if I didn't let myself be taken by the female. But then there was the question of why did the female want me?

"No!" I said. "Humans are despicable, horrible and disgusting creatures! I'd rather die before I let one take me."

"That can be arranged," Highhead said, a glint in his pale gray-blue eyes. He started to advance on me, his crest twitching, first up, then down, then up, then down. I heard a *tap-tap* sound, and looked down to see his talons tapping on the floor.

"What would Father say?" I asked. "Oh, by the way, he's right behind you." The Eagletish trick worked. Highhead's eyes widened, his pupils dilating in fear. He backed away from me, and looked over his shoulder—

And then I was gone. I forced myself to believe what I was doing was right, and I circled, spotting the female. She was holding a length of black material.

Browntuft was there, too. He seemed to have guessed my plan, following me. "Swiftwing!" he screeched. "Don't do this!" Jago shot a bullet at him, but missed. Browntuft hissed and flew away, alighting on another branch.

I circled down slowly, landing on a tree near the Human. I still held back.

I didn't need to, because suddenly, the girl was there, in the tree. How she had gotten up, I didn't know, but there she was. She was actually quite pretty and tall for her age, maybe twelve or so years old. The black material was actually a hood, shaped like my head.

I closed my eyes, waiting for the inevitable. I heard Browntuft screech, somewhere far off, and my eyes flickered open for a second. He was diving right at me.

And then the Human slipped the hood over my eyes.

Part II

Browntuft, the Philippine Hawk-Eagle

CHAPTER 14

A BAIT

I watched, horrified, as the female Human climbed down from the tree with Swiftwing in her arms. She dropped to the ground and ran to Jago, the Human that had shot Swiftwing. No. No. No. No. This could *not* be happening! Not Swiftwing, my best friend who had comforted me when I had been lost. And now, she was the one who was lost. The forest blurred into the background as I stayed, perched on the tree near the edge of the clearing, watching Swiftwing getting taken away. I started to pant. The safety I had felt with Swiftwing around faded. I started to feel the world enclosing on me.

Jago patted the female human on the back, shifted the black hood on Swiftwing's head, and then slung her over his shoulder like she was a sack of something useless. Anger shot through my wings, and I wanted to rush at Jago. But it was too late, and he probably could have fended me off anyway. And it would do no good to Swiftwing if I died, right after she got captured.

As I watched the proceedings, I realized that I couldn't always rely on Swiftwing, especially now that she was gone. I would have to grow bolder and stronger. I would have to grow up. I had to change.

I followed them as they trudged off into the rainforest. Flying feathers, they looked terribly clumsy, stumbling over every small stone or vine in their path. My conscience told me to help them, pull the vines out of their path; lead them out of this forest. But something warned me not to. I realized what it was when Jago took out a long rifle and pointed it at a small furry shape. He aimed and let the bullet loose. It hit the furry shape and the animal fell to the ground, a small squeak coming from its mouth. It was a giant cloud rat.

Jago raced forwards and grabbed the rodent, dangling it in the air by its tail. When he saw it was only a cloud rat, he made a sound of dismissal and threw it into the bushes. The female exclaimed something, and Jago looked at her, his flint-like eyes glaring. He called the female "Althea."

My short crest went up, watching the Human shoot an animal and then throw it away. Sure, it was food, but I was pretty sure that Humans didn't eat cloud rats. *They eat cooked meat*, according to many legends.

Jago went on to insult Althea. He pointed to himself and then said, "Poacher." Flying feathers! What did that mean? Were Swiftwing and I wrong? Was his name not Jago, but Poacher? *Don't doubt Swiftwing*, I thought. I took a deep breath, and realized: His name *was* Jago, but the Human group he was in was called "The Poachers."

I ruffled my feathers in agitation as I watched Jago drop Swiftwing on the forest floor. He let a Human laugh and then picked her up, throwing her over his shoulder again. He continued tromping off towards the edge of the rainforest, with Althea stumbling to keep up behind him.

§   §   §

I flew back to the Philippine Eagles' Aerie, my heart in my throat. Trees loomed, bigger than before and more terrifying, like I might crash into them. What would happen to Swiftwing now that the Humans had her? I knew that Philippine Eagles were super rare, so Humans probably wouldn't kill her, but they might hurt her. I couldn't stand the thought of them taking her captive in one of those metal cages that I'd heard about.

I arrived in the clearing in the woods. Fierceheart, Swiftwing's father, was waiting for me, flying in circles around the clearing. When he saw me, he soared towards me so quickly that he almost didn't stop. Just in time, he veered up and landed on a nearby tree. I circled for a moment, and then landed next to him. I could see how Swiftwing resembled her father. There was this look in her eyes—a lot like Swiftwing's. A fighter. He was striking and quite big for a male.

"Where's the Human taking her?" asked Fierceheart.

"I don't know," I replied.

A flash of anger overcame his features. He raised one of his talons threateningly. "Don't insult me," he warned. "Swiftwing may like you, but I have no reason to trust you, and it does not help if you tease me. Either way, did she look safe, or should we follow her?" He put his talon into a large gash in a tree, coating it with sap, his crest going up.

"I'm sorry!" I said, rushing to soothe him. "I didn't mean anything!

But she seemed pretty safe." I didn't try to ask why he had coated his talons with sap.

Fierceheart's eyes narrowed, and he leaned in. "I don't believe you." I felt a flash of resentment. "But, we don't need to act right away then. Good. I hope you don't insult me again."

Flying feathers! I didn't insult important birds. I knew that it was wrong, and so I didn't do it. It was as simple as that. But Swiftwing's father here had to question my politeness!

"I assure you, I meant nothing by it," I said icily. Fierceheart looked surprised, and I felt the same. I had just thought that I was polite, and then here I was, talking back. "Sorry," I said. "I'd better go tell Swiftwing's mother—"

"I'll tell her," suggested Fierceheart. Or at least, it sounded like a suggestion. The warm tone, the way the end of the "her" went up slightly and the tilt of his head. But the dark glint in his eyes told me that it was an order. "Are you going to fly away?" he asked.

"Yes, of course!" I said, thinking, *Flying feathers, isn't it obvious?* "I need to stretch my wings, you know." I lifted my wings, showing them to Fierceheart. Along with showing him my wings, I felt the urge to feel bigger. I straightened my legs a little. Like Fierceheart sensed what I was doing, he himself puffed up his crest, dominating over me.

"Wrong answer." Before I could question his statement, the talon coated with sap flashed out and scraped the length of both of my under-wings. Instinctively, I closed my wings, but it was too late. He had already stuck the sap on, and so when I tried to free my wings, I found they were stuck to me. "Try to free that and you'll rip out most of your feathers," said Fierceheart, sounding satisfied.

"Why?" I asked. "Are—" then I realized it. Fierceheart hated other species of birds. It was the only way I could explain the way he acted around me compared to the way he acted with his own kind. And he probably didn't trust me that much, either. After all, I had been friends with Swiftwing for a dry season, and then she got captured.

As if reading my mind—"Exactly," he said.

§　　§　　§

I stayed there for a long time. What had I done to deserve this? It had only started because I was small...

I remembered the Leader, Silentflight, sneering as he pointed at me with his talon. "That one," he had said, his gray-brown beak twisting. "That runt."

I had taken off then. In complete disregard of the rules, in complete disgrace of everything I believed in, I had jumped off.

I found myself panting right now, thinking about what I had done. I needed to stop this nightmare right now! Instead, the memories came flooding back, even stronger.

Flying feathers! I had a sudden adrenaline rush. My wings pumped, trying to gain height, as Silentflight's Advisors gained on me, their gray beaks snapping cruelly.

I had screeched and landed on a tree. Silentflight was there suddenly. He wasn't called what he was for nothing. He started walking towards me, along the length of the branch.

"You thought you could escape me?" he'd asked. I'd whirled around, ready to escape that way, but his helpers were obstructing that way. So I looked up at the sky, only to see Hawk-Eagle bodies blocking my view, blocking the only escape route. "No killing," said Silentflight, starting to advance on me. "But no bird said anything about maiming." He lashed out with his talon.

A voice shook me from my thoughts. "What are you doing here,

Hawk-Eagle?" snarled Highhead. "I could use it..." he muttered to himself. "To torture you..."

"Nutbrain!" I screeched in horror, shying away from him.

He only hissed in laughter and stared at me mockingly. "I'm bigger than you," he said. "You can't defeat me."

"No, I can't," I said, smiling in spite of myself, "But maybe Fierceheart can." It was all clear now. It had been a ruse. I didn't think Fierceheart actually hated me *that* much, and I had been right. It had just been to lure Highhead out in the first place!

Highhead gaped at me, as if realizing the same thing, his eyes bugging out, then slowly turned around. Fierceheart, his crest raised, let out a screech and launched himself at Highhead.

CHAPTER 15

MIXED-ROLE

Highhead looked up, his eyes slitted. His wings were glued to his sides by the same gummy paste that had restrained me. His dark brown wings jerked, almost madly as he spoke. His eyes, dark blue, so dark almost black, moved from side to side.

"I said no torture, and I meant it," began Fierceheart. "So what were you doing with the Philippine Hawk-Eagle?"

"The name's Browntuft," I hissed under my breath.

Suddenly, one of Highhead's wings swept out. A lot of his

feathers had been ripped in half, damaged by when he had pulled it free of the restraining sap, but he still seemed strong. His other wing came up, knocking Fierceheart off the platform.

Scarletcrest must have been in on the plan. She jumped up from the platform and started attacking birds that tried to help me. Silverneck dodged one of Highhead's talons and then flew off the platform.

Sharpbeak, being loyal to his father, copied Scarletcrest, starting to fend off other Eagles that tried to help the Leader. Longtalon swept under Highhead's wing and raked his claws along his stomach, but a blow to his head sent him crashing away.

"Yield!" shouted Fierceheart, flying up. Grayspan, Lightfeather's mate, seemed to fall right into his element. He spun around like a torpedo for a moment, and then dodged Highhead's snapping beak, scratching Highhead's wing. As Highhead looked at his wound, Grayspan seized the opportunity and swung his wing to hit Highhead. However, Highhead still managed to duck and Grayspan's momentum threw him into a tree, where he crumpled to the ground. Highhead, freeing his other wing, flew off the platform. He circled, then came down, landing on Fierceheart. Then my vision became purple.

§   §   §

The next thing I knew, I was standing on Highhead's chest. His eyes were closed, his head bleeding, and his wings were astray. A lot of his feathers were strewn all over the place.

"What did you do?" screeched Scarletcrest. She flew over to me, looking horrified. "You killed him!" I checked his heartbeat, putting one of my talons on his chest. His pulse was there, but very weak.

"Sorry," I said. "I didn't kill him. I don't even know what happened."

"Well, it was...surprising," said Fierceheart. His eyes were wide, his crest flared.

"You sort of flew into a rage," commented Sharpbeak.

"What? I never fly into a rage!" I said, preening my feathers. A lot of Highhead's feathers were stuck in my talons, so I had to work them out. "I'm more of a Hunter, sorry." I realized what Fierceheart said—he didn't seem like he was lying. I started to frown.

"What's happening to me?" I asked.

Scarletcrest shrugged, refolding her wings in. "I wouldn't know. But Fierceheart might. By the way," she said, "do you want to know what happened to Highhead?"

Fierceheart interrupted her. "After Highhead jumped on me, you went berserk and soared at him, grabbing him and flipping him over. You ripped out many of his wing-feathers and hit him in the head with your talons countless times. Then you finally knocked him unconscious. It was odd. You seemed bigger when you fought him. You also managed to dodge all of the trees better than a Warrior could. The trees seemed to not be there at all!"

"What?" I asked. "I want to be a Hunter, like Swiftwing. I'm no Warrior."

"Unless—" started Fierceheart. "It's rare." He cleared his throat, looking down at his talons.

"What's rare?"

Fierceheart looked at me. He seemed slightly annoyed, like I had interrupted an important trail of thought. "Do you know what the rules about mixed-roles are?" he asked.

When I dipped my head, he stared down at me.

"Yes," I said. "You can be a Warrior and a Healer at the same time, or a Hunter-Healer, or a Warrior-Hunter."

"The latter is the most common, if mixed-roles takes place at all," he said. "Known birds that had mixed-roles were few. The most recent was a Philippine Hawk-Eagle called Palechest, who I'm sure you know."

I gaped at Swiftwing's father. He seemed excited and triumphant, like he was wondering if he was correct. I couldn't believe he knew.

"Palechest was my father," I gasped. "He died. He was well-known."

Fierceheart's eyes widened for a moment, and then it was like his moment of surprise had never happened. "Of course," he said smoothly, sweeping his wing along the platform in an elegant gesture. "You see, mixed-roles usually come from parents, which leads me to believe that you will have a mixed-role. What roles did your father have?"

"Warrior and Healer."

"What did I tell you?" asked Fierceheart. He looked up at the sky, a figure of pride and importance. "Then you'll either be a Hunter-Healer or a Warrior-Hunter. And as I screeched before, the latter is the usual."

Highhead began to stir under me. I had forgotten to get off him. His first sweep of the wing knocked me off, and the second was after he had gotten up, and it was aimed at my head. However, the most surprising bird blocked it. Scarletcrest held up her wing and knocked Highhead's aside. She followed this with a scratch at her mate's stomach.

"What?" asked Highhead blearily. He peered up at Scarletcrest, and then his eyes widened. "Traitor!"

"No, Advisor," interjected Scarletcrest, looking coolly at her mate. She was bigger, so she added to the insult by overshadowing Highhead. "You're the traitor, for you disobeyed the law of the Aeries to not torture other species, and you'll be cast out. You tried to chase out Browntuft for being a different species. That's crime enough."

"What? No!" screamed Highhead. He started kicking and snapping his beak, trying to free himself. I felt a pang of pity for a moment, but it was replaced with revulsion. Sure, Scarletcrest had attacked her mate, but only for a good reason. Highhead was struggling against her for a bad one.

"You are hereby—" started Fierceheart, but he was interrupted by a bout of screeching from Highhead. He took a deep breath, looking impatient. "As I said, Highhead, you are hereby exiled from the Aerie."

Highhead stopped. He stared at the circle of birds surrounding him. He looked surprised, as if he'd never thought that he would be exiled from his Aerie. "What? You can't—Scarletcrest!" he screeched.

"Too late," said his mate, sounding sympathetic. "I want a loyal Philippine Eagle to take care of my eaglets, not a traitor. Ready, Silverneck?"

The Advisor nodded, and both stepped forward. They grabbed him, Scarletcrest gripping his shoulders, and then Fierceheart moved forward, and put some sap on Highhead's wings. The two Advisors both flew into the forest at the edge of the clearing, Highhead still screeching abuse at his mate. Finally, they dropped him. He crashed through multiple layers of branches before his screeches grew silent.

§　　§　　§

"Well, that's that," said Fierceheart, sighing. "Highhead was a fierce Warrior, but it doesn't matter if his spirit isn't good. May the Ibon Spirit curse him."

I stared at the Leader. That was the worst curse in the history of the Philippine Aeries! I wondered what would happen to Highhead now that the curse had fallen on him, and felt a bit of sadness for him. He could have been a good Warrior, maybe even a Leader. And then he had to ruin it for himself.

I sighed. "You're right. He really could have been good." I didn't add my thought about him being a Leader. "That's it now. We won't see him again."

Just then, Scarletcrest and Silverneck flew in. Scarletcrest was heaving. "Highhead sure was heavy," she said. Her crest was slightly up; she was obviously distressed. "I always had a suspicion that he was insubordinate." She saw me staring at the Leader. "What did he do?" she asked, sounding wary.

"He cast the Ibon's curse on him."

"Who and whom?"

"Fierceheart cast it on Highhead."

Scarletcrest gave a plaintive little whine. "No!" she screeched. "Highhead was bad, but he didn't deserve *that*! Oh, slash it. Now Fierceheart can't take it back." I had an image of Highhead lying dead, flies and maggots swarming around him. I blinked once, and the image disappeared.

"Right," I said. "I need to drink." I was aware of the aching, burning thirst in my throat. I hadn't drank in a really long time. "Do you know where the water is?"

"Little spring northeast," said Scarletcrest, pointing in the direction. Her eyes were looking in a different direction, though. She seemed distracted. She started scratching the platform under her talons.

I flew north, and let out a sigh of relief when I saw clear water bubbling out of a small rock wall, like a spot of turquoise in a sea of green. Monkeys, chittering, moved out of the way and swung into the forest when they saw me, orange blurs and flashes.

Quite a large pool had gathered under the spring, and long, sweeping branches hung over the water. The water itself was warm and turquoise colored. I landed on a fallen branch near the edge of the spring-fed pool, dipped my beak in the warm water, and started to drink, sucking in the water. It was warm, but still refreshed me. I turned around, ready to fly away, spreading my wings.

That was when the ground started to shake under me.

CHAPTER 16

EARTHQUAKE

I screeched as I was thrown off balance, falling into the warm water. The water kept me down, and I could feel it drenching my wings, soaking, heavy, cumbersome. I surged up quickly, my mind searching for words that would explain the rumble. Storm? No. Tidal wave? No. *Earthquake.* I could find nothing wrong with that explanation. On the ground? Check. Ground moving? Check. Rumbling? Check.

My wings were too wet to fly right away, so I waited for a moment, and then found a thermal updraft and soared back to the Philippine

Eagles' Aerie. Up in the air, I could still be targeted by the earthquake. The shakings of the ground caused trees to sway violently, creating wind that tossed me off course. Everything was chaotic. I could hardly concentrate on flying, much less dodging the tree trunks.

Somehow I managed to work my way back to the Aerie, my wings still damp from my fall into the river. I had lost countless feathers; some on trees, bushes or twigs. In the end, I felt exhausted, but I had arrived on the Bent-branch tree.

"Browntuft?" asked a familiar voice. I found myself staring into Fierceheart's formidable gray-blue eyes, except they didn't seem formidable, they seemed scared.

"Listen," he said. "Swiftwing is the future of the Aerie. I want you to look for her and report back." He glared at me as if daring me to contradict him.

"Will you throw me off a tree and mourn my death?" I asked, worried that I wouldn't be accepted into the Ibon afterlife.

Fierceheart held my gaze for a moment. Then he looked down at his talons, embarrassed. "Fine," he said. "*If* you die."

"I probably will," I commented. "When do I go?"

Fierceheart leveled me with a hard glare. "Now."

"How do I get up?" I asked, standing at the edge of the platform. "I feel no hot air."

"There's one right next to you, nutbrain," snapped Fierceheart.

I looked down, but could see nothing except for a giant crack from the earthquake that had hot air blowing out of it.

I realized what that meant. *Aha!* I thought. *The cracks are hot air!* I positioned myself above one of the spouts of air pushing up, and started flapping. I slowly rose above the platform, and then flew north. I felt amazing, or at least, I would have, had it not been for a huge tree that started to shake.

The tree gave a groan, the roots ripping out of the soil, as the quaking ground underneath started to slide. Loose rocks and clods of dirt were spat into the humid air, and the tree slid down the steep slope. Then it fell, its branches aimed right at me. The wind knocked me to the ground.

I rolled out of the way and barely escaped the trunk. Loud splintering and breaking sounds filled the air, and so did a loud shriek of pain. Who...? I looked at myself, and saw that one of my wings was pinned under a small branch, and it was scratched up, feathers missing. Ah...I must have been the one to scream. I yanked my wing out from under the tree, and screeched again when a few of my feathers were ripped out.

"Ow," I whimpered. I stalked over to a crack, every step hurting me, and then used the updraft to fly up. Instantly, I felt like I was on fire. Every time I moved my wing I wanted to scream, but I gritted my beak, thinking, *I will not shriek I will not shriek I will not shriek*—my trail of thought ended when I rammed into a good-sized tree and fell down, the pain consuming me. Just as I was about to hit the ground, I swooped out of my fall.

"Ow," I repeated, but I didn't mean it any less. I resolved to walk the rest of the way. After a few minutes of walking, I unfurled my wing. It didn't hurt anymore. It had scabbed over.

Even though I didn't like Fierceheart, I definitely liked Swiftwing. That was what drove me on, made me use an updraft and start flying. I was so tired, so fatigued, but I continued on northward, hearing my own labored breathing. The forest seemed darker and warmer, and a blanket of mist had settled.

I landed near a spring of water. This one was far smaller than the one that I had been at the beginning of the earthquake, and it was cloudy. However, I dipped my beak in the warm water and drank most of the little pool. I spread my wings, ready to fly away, when a voice sounded behind me.

"Just where do you think you're going?"

§   §   §

I turned around, fear coursing through my veins. Oh no . . . I could see nothing except for foliage when I turned my head, however. Maybe I had imagined it? Then an entire flock of birds emerged from the trees and bushes behind me. My heart started to beat, me panting as I watched the birds advance on me. I couldn't fight them off.

The first thing, and the only, that I noted about them, was that these weren't Philippine Eagles. These were Philippine Serpent Eagles, and legend said that it didn't do well to anger these fierce birds. To Philippine Eagles they were tiny, minuscule even, but to Philippine Hawk-Eagles, they were only a little smaller. For a full grown, my species was a head taller, but since I was still juvenile, they towered over me. They ate snakes, like their name, and I stared at them in disgust. Then the lead one spoke. Something in me had twisted my feelings for them, finding it hard to believe that they could speak; that they were individuals, that there was someone in them. Now I listened.

"Who are you?" asked the one in the lead in Philippine bird-speak. He seemed to be bigger than the rest. He dominated over me.

"My name is Browntuft," I said.

The one in the lead turned to his flock and conferred with them in Philippine Serpent Eagle-speak. It had never occurred to me, but the Philippine Eagles I had been with could have always just talked to themselves in Philippine Eagle-speak, but they had chosen to use Philippine bird-speak. Most birds used normal bird-speak unless they wanted to keep something a secret—like right now.

"That is not enough," said the one in the lead. He had a brown body with dull white spots, like most Philippine Serpent Eagles, but his beak had no yellow on it was entirely gray. His eyes were the usual, though, a dark golden-brown. "I shall tell you my name is Dullsnap. Does that tell you anything?"

I shook my head, trying not to show my fear. "I am a Philippine Hawk-Eagle."

"And I am a Philippine Serpent Eagle. Does that change your mind about me?"

"I am about two and half years old."

"And I am twenty years old. Does that make you trust me more?"

"I am small."

"And I am big. Does that make you want to agree with me?"

"I am friends with Philippine Eagles!" I snapped, tired of the amused looks that the Philippine Serpent Eagles were giving me. For a moment, the leader actually seemed surprised. His beak was slightly open. Then he closed it with a snap.

"Of course you are," he crooned softly. "And I am friends with my Leader. Does that tell you that you should listen to me and not tell lies?" He raked his talon along the floor, leaving three deep trenches.

I was about to shake my head when he met my eyes and narrowed his. Something in his glare made me say, "Yes. But I told you the truth about me."

"In our Aerie, lies are not tolerated," said Dullsnap. "If you were part of our Aerie, then you would be punished."

"Okay," I said quietly. "Take me to your Leader, then." Flying feathers, what was wrong with me? And why didn't I run?

He signaled to one of the other Serpent Eagles. "Pick up Browntuft and blindfold him with a leaf. If he struggles, feel free to knock him unconscious. But don't harm him." I was tempted to ask whether or not knocking me out counted as harming me, but I bit my beak shut.

CHAPTER 17

A DETOUR

I sat in a large tree, thinking, *What have I done to deserve this?* I tried to remember everything that had happened. Fierceheart, if I ever returned, would like to know about an enemy's territory. I hadn't been able to see, with the large leaf that covered my entire face down to the beak, but I could still hear. There were a lot of birds in this Aerie, though. I could tell that by listening.

I also knew that the forest was dense in this part. I had felt the leaves brushing me on either side of my body and the painful sensation of brushing against a rather spiky or rough tree too many times. I was sure I would leave feathers on protruding broken branches. Every so often, Dullsnap snapped at somebird behind him.

That was all good information about the Serpent Eagle's Aerie. There were a lot of birds, they had a dense forest, and they used leaves to blindfold enemies. I would have to tell Fierceheart that, except it led to one thought that I didn't want to dwell on. *What if I don't get out of this alive? Or at all?*

I felt feathers scratch my cheek as a bird flew past me. I could hear what it was talking about.

" Did you see the Human training the Philippine Eagle at the edge of the forest? Any respectable Eagle wouldn't allow that to happen."

I felt a surge of excitement. Flying feathers! I tapped my claws along the nest I was on, trying to let loose my jitteriness. There was only one bird that I knew who had been captured by a Human and was a Philippine Eagle, and that was Swiftwing.

§ § §

I didn't know if I should shriek in sadness or be elated. It was a good thing she was alive, but the fact that a Human was training her? Had she even allowed it? As far as I knew, Humans didn't train birds, and if they wanted to, they forced the bird to agree.

There was a thud and *whoosh* of wings as a bird landed on my platform and folded his wings in. I couldn't see him, but somehow I knew it was Dullsnap. A talon reached out and pulled the leaf of my eyes, and I got my first glimpse of the Aerie.

As I had noticed before, it did have many birds. So many, in fact, I couldn't count them. They nested on the same stick platforms that many raptors used. There were so many, and it didn't help that they all had white dots over their body, blending them in so it was like they were a moving wave. I had heard here that there were more Hunters than Warriors, with so many eaglets to feed.

I asked, "Can't I fly away?"

Dullsnap looked at me grimly. "Maybe if you knew the way back."

"I do!" I said. "So can I go?"

"Well then, how do you get back?"

"You fly east. Wait. No, south. Actually, maybe north." I spun around. "Yeah."

Dullsnap cocked his head and dropped something at my feet. "Food," he said.

I looked down at his gift and saw what looked like a limp, scaly rope. Then I realized it was a snake.

Dullsnap nudged the reptile closer to me. "Eat."

"Flying feathers, is that a snake?" I exclaimed. I backed away from the animal. It had been killed with the stomp-and-shake method, so it was slightly flattened.

"Yes," said Dullsnap, narrowing his eyes at me. "And we expect you to eat it, Browntuft." Flying feathers, he'd said my name again! These birds weren't too bad.

"Uh...I don't eat snakes," I said. "I eat palm civets, squirrels, mice if I have to, cloud rats are okay, voles can be a treat."

As I said "palm civets," he looked away, grimacing. When I said, "squirrels," his eyes widened. After I told him, "mice if I have to," he dipped his head, like he agreed that he would only eat them if he "had to." When I commented that cloud rats were okay, he looked like he might die of disgust. Flying feathers, when I said, "voles can be a treat," he actually backed away from me and spread his wings like he wanted to fly away!

"You. Have. Horrible. Taste," said Dullsnap, looking longingly at a nest in a nearby tree. It was probably his family's. "If you won't eat a snake, then a lizard?" He flew away and a moment later came back with a small striped lizard. "Or—" He jumped off my platform again and returned with a much smaller snake—"a smaller snake! Here's how you eat it." Dullsnap brought the larger serpent to his beak. He opened it wide, then started eating the snake.

Flying feathers! It was odd how he ate. He didn't seem to rip it apart. He started swallowing it, and it looked like a long, scaly tongue that he was slowly sucking in. He closed his beak with a sharp snap, sucked in the remaining tail, then swallowed.

"That was filling," he said. "I find it hard to believe that you could actually finish a snake by yourself, you being small." A sound of amusement emerged from his beak.

"Right," I said. "Can I hunt for myself then?"

"Can you?" asked Dullsnap. He narrowed his eyes. "Aren't you too small?"

"No, I can! Flying feathers, are you actually saying—"

"I am," said Dullsnap, approaching. He pulled the remains of the leaf off my face. "If you want, you can try to hunt, but promise that you'll return."

For a moment, I had thoughts of escaping and never coming back. But it would feel just so wrong to deceive these birds that actually treated other birds with respect. After all, if I tricked them, I might not have the warm welcome I would hope for if I ever came back. "Fine," I said. "I promise."

"Very well," replied Dullsnap. His eyes started to twinkle. "You don't want to see your Philippine Eagle friend?" His voice dripped with sarcasm.

"Flying feathers, what?" I cried. I advanced on him. "You didn't tell me—flying feathers—can I see?" *Swiftwing!* I thought. *I'll be able to see the Human training you!* Another thought overwhelmed that one, though— *But why are you even letting that Human train you?*

"What are you thinking?" asked Dullsnap. He craned his neck, looking at my downcast face. "You seem sad, but you seem happy."

"It's just," I choked out, "the Philippine Eagle that the Human's training—I know her." Dullsnap stared at me in shock.

"What do you mean?" he questioned. "Ah, you're joking. I see."

"I'm not!" I cried.

Dullsnap's eyes widened, and he leaned into me until our crests were almost touching.

"I see," he repeated. "I see. I'll take you to see them, then. Are you sure you don't want to eat anything?"

"No," I said, feeling my heartbeat start to speed up. I raised my crest so fast that Dullsnap had to back away. *Tap tap tap*—I looked down to see my talons tapping against the platform.

"Alright!" said Dullsnap. He opened his wings and took off quickly, and I followed him.

§ § §

A few minutes later we landed on the floor near a bunch of bushes. Flying feathers, those things were humongous! They covered most of the floor of the Philippine Serpent Eagle Aerie. They also looked monstrous—sharp, thorny tangles, clusters of small, mauve berries that looked poisonous, spiked, jagged, dark green leaves. However, it gave off an air of beauty, somehow.

"Flying feathers," I murmured to myself, staring in awe at the huge bramble ahead of me. The flock of birds that herded me there settled down, and so did I, trying to erase thoughts of escape.

"Where is Browntuft?" asked one of the Serpent Eagles. "Where is—"

"Here," I said. "The real question is: Where is Swiftwing?"

"Swiftwing who?" asked Dullsnap, stalking towards me. "Who is that?"

"My Philippine Eagle friend," I said, trying to ignore the stares and rasps around me. I could tell that while some of them were surprised or even horrified, most were intrigued.

"She's coming," said the same Serpent Eagle that had asked me where I was. He walked forward and pulled a curtain of leaves away from a spot in the large bushes. I peered through the hole.

What I first saw was the Human, Althea. Then I saw the next thing: a bird. My vision tunneled on Swiftwing, the Philippine Eagle, and my only friend.

CHAPTER 18

REUNION

"Swiftwing!" I called out softly, not wanting to alert the female Human I was there. Swiftwing gave no sign that she had heard me. Then her crest went up and flicked in my direction. *Yes!*

Flying feathers—she was standing on the Human's arm! The arm itself was covered with thick, burlap cloth. Swiftwing's talons were tied with rope, and Althea's gloved fingers were gripping the rope so she couldn't escape. The rope was blue and striped.

As I watched, Althea let go of the rope and made a throwing

motion in a random direction. Swiftwing jumped up, and the momentum carried her forward. She paused, gliding, and I could imagine her thinking what to do. Flying feathers, why was she even listening to the Human? Why not fly away?

Swiftwing seemed to finish thinking and she dived towards the bushes. The entire place was a grassy clearing, much like the clearing in the Philippine Eagle Aerie. Where were we? I looked away for a moment, to see the rest of the place, and when I looked back, Swiftwing was standing on a tree at the edge of the clearing.

Now I didn't care if Althea saw me. Flying feathers, she could cut off my wings and that wouldn't stop me from talking to Swiftwing again. "Swiftwing!" I screamed, this time much louder.

She had already seen me, but Swiftwing still looked surprised and excited. "Is that really you?" asked Swiftwing. Her voice was high pitched with...sadness? Excitement? Surprise?

"It's me!" I called. I flew up to the branch she was on. "Swiftwing, is it you, or is it another Eagle?" I was just making sure. My heart beat with excitement.

"It's me," screeched Swiftwing. "I missed you so much. Great Ibon

Spirit, I couldn't live another day without talking to another bird." She raked the branch under her feet, and pieces of soft inner bark rained down on the Eagles below.

"The Serpent Eagles brought me here, and Highhead's been exiled, and...right! How's your wound?" I asked.

"Althea applied some paste, and used some type of patch to cover it up. It still hurts a little, but other than that it's all good."

I smiled at her. "It's awesome you're healed, but why are you letting the Human train you?"

Swiftwing shuddered. "Jago would jab something at me if I didn't. The first day I was aching all over.."

Althea screamed, "Eagle, come back here, please!"

I was surprised that she was so polite.

Wait.

What?

I could understand her?

§   §   §

"Swiftwing," I panted. "Did that just happen, or is it just me?"

"What?" Swiftwing asked, looking down at the ground. She preened her feathers like nothing had happened.

"What do you mean, *what*?" I asked angrily. I scratched the bark of the tree, agitated. "That's not nothing! Althea was talking in bird-speak!"

"And she can understand me too," said Swiftwing, blinking her eyes sarcastically. "Did the Serpent Eagles hit your head? Great Ibon Spirit, if they did…"

As much as I was pleased that she cared about me that much, my frustration with her disbelief outweighed it. "No, I can understand her! She said, 'Eagle, come back here, please!'"

"Then I guess I should," said Swiftwing. She closed her eyes for a moment. "But the fact that you can understand her—that's not unheard of." She flashed her wings out once, then brought them in again.

Back in the meadow, Althea was screaming for Swiftwing. Flying feathers—I caught the word "bat" in her speech! Somehow, I knew that those were the prodding things that Jago poked Swiftwing with.

"Flying feathers! They're going to poke you if you don't come back in…" I concentrated on finding out what else she was saying. "If you don't come back in five seconds. Which, by the way, are heartbeats."

Swiftwing screeched in laughter, and she flicked one of her wings across my body. "Great Ibon Spirit, calm down," she laughed. "You made up a joke when I was gone?"

"No," I replied, shifting nervously.

"Then be quiet, we're meeting, and you're ruining it," said Swiftwing. She scratched her talon on the bark, and brown scraps fell off and on to the bushes below, speckling them brown. Speaking of below, I craned my neck and chanced a glance underneath us. I saw the Serpent Eagles milling around, sometimes staring up at Swiftwing and me in shock. Every few heartbeats, one would point at us. Their white spots flashed and distracted me. I turned to Swiftwing.

"Flying feathers!" I screeched. "They'll poke you with a bat." Swiftwing made a screech of amusement and then looked at my face.

"Bat?" she asked. "What's a bat? Great Ibon Spirit, those Serpent Eagles. They hit your head hard!" She trailed off, looking at the Aerie meandering below. Then she looked back up at me. "Honestly, I said before it's not unheard of, and I think that you might be a Human-whisperer."

"What's that?"

"Popular legends," said Swiftwing, lowering her voice to a rasp, darting a glance down at the Serpent Eagles. "Not popular, actually. Obscure. But legend has it that every few centuries there will be a bird that can understand Humans, and Humans can understand it. Go on, try to speak to Althea."

Now I was the one who thought that Swiftwing had hit her head. "Well, it can't hurt," I said, then retucked my wings under my chest. I preened myself, subconsciously trying to make myself look better for the Human. I stopped myself as my beak was halfway to my chest. *Flying feathers, Browntuft, they're Humans!* I thought. But that didn't stop me from preening. I brushed all of the last few days' grime that I had accumulated, making my feathers soft. Then I called out to the Human, "Althea, can you understand me?"

I tapped my talons against the branch quickly, then forced myself to stop. There was no way this was going to work...right? I had a nagging feeling at my stomach, like my prey was alive and walking around in it. If this worked, then I would make up for my size. All the comments that my former Aerie had thrown my way would mean nothing. My heart started to burst in my chest as I watched Althea. My vision tunneled until the only thing I saw was her.

I was hoping, hoping with all my strength, all my heart, all my mind, that this would work. My former skepticism had been replaced with hope.

Then Althea turned across the meadow and gaped at me.

§   §   §

I stared at Swiftwing, and she looked back at me, her expression conveying her shock.

"What?" Swiftwing asked, her tone slightly higher, like she was trying to restrain from screeching in surprise. The earthquake had stopped a long time ago, but I still felt like the tree was shaking under me. I would finally be more than just a runt! The bully's teasing in my former Aerie would just be fluff!

"Flying feathers! That—that worked!" I screamed, glaring at Swiftwing. In the meadow, Althea clutched her head, rolling over the floor. She was alone, so she had no reason to talk, but she was screaming at the sky. If I listened harder, I could hear her.

"That's so crazy! So not real!" She pinched herself, then doubled over, rubbing the red spot on her arm.

"What is she saying?" asked Swiftwing sarcastically. When I ignored her, "No, seriously!" she screeched.

"She said, 'That's so crazy! So not real!'" I quoted. Swiftwing looked almost as shocked as Althea, who was now getting up and slapping herself in the face, muttering words to herself.

"You sure?" Swiftwing asked, walking closer to me. My heart beat angrily, because she didn't believe me.

"Yes!"

Swiftwing narrowed her eyes for a moment. Then she sighed and backed down. "I believe you," she said.

My heart skipped a beat this time. I felt relieved that she finally, actually believed me. Flying feathers, it was really annoying when someone kept doubting you—especially if that someone was your only friend!

"Good," I said. "How? How does it work?" For some reason, I wasn't really surprised. It was like I knew it, but I was just waiting for it to be confirmed.

A grim expression crossed Swiftwing's face. She narrowed her eyes, but she wasn't looking at me, she was looking at the sky.

"The Ibon Spirit," she said stiffly, glaring at the sun. "Legend says that the Ibon Spirit can gift birds so that they can talk or understand Humans, but usually it's just Eagle Owls."

I scraped my talon along the tree we were on, glancing at the Serpent Eagles. The few left watching us looked bored. As I looked on, I saw three Eagles lift off and fly back to the center of their Aerie. The feathers on their back moved as they flexed their legs and pumped their wings. Another two followed, leaving only three. And then those three, including Dullsnap, soared away.

"Why are you angry at the Ibon Spirit?" I asked. I blinked at Swiftwing. Flying feathers, it was horrible to be angry at the Ibon Spirit! Why—?

Swiftwing answered my flood of thoughts when she next spoke. "The Ibon Spirit was the reason I was exiled, Browntuft."

"Flying feathers! Directly or indirectly?"

"Guess what!" snapped Swiftwing angrily at me. "It wasn't there at all, but Keeneye kept on saying it wouldn't like me! And it didn't argue!" She turned away from me, preening her feathers.

I retucked my wings under my chest, then shifted them so they went over. "So indirectly," I guessed, not waiting for her response. Down on the floor, I watched as Dullsnap flew back, followed by several other Eagles. He swerved around some vines and dodged a tree.

Dullsnap flew up the tree, landed next to Swiftwing, and said, "My Leader's back now. You should go see him. Philippine Eagle, you can go."

"It's Swiftwing," said Swiftwing, and I could tell she didn't think that Dullsnap would listen. Instead, he only said,

"Okay, Swiftwing, you can go."

"Bye, Browntuft. I will go to my Aerie as soon as I can," said Swiftwing. "That is, if Althea lets me. But she probably will."

"Bye, Swiftwing," I said. Then I followed Dullsnap back to his Aerie.

CHAPTER 19

A MISSION

Alittle while later, I sat on the platform of the Leader of the Philippine Serpent Eagle Aerie.

"What is your name?" asked the Leader. Flying feathers, it was going to happen again! I was going to be tricked into saying a bunch of sentences that didn't make any sense, like what Dullsnap had done to me.

"My name is Browntuft, I am a Philippine Hawk-Eagle, I am two and half years of age, and I am friends with a Philippine Eagle," I said in one gasp.

"And that's why I called you to be here," he said. "Knowing that you're friends with a Philippine Eagle, we want you to broker peace between our two Aeries."

"Why would I want to do that?" I asked, cocking my head.

"You do know that Keeneye died, right?" he retorted.

"Flying feathers, of course I do!"

"Well, she was helping one of our Eaglets when there was an unfortunate accident, and we were blamed for it."

"What happened?" I was about to ask before Dullsnap interjected.

"You might not have known this, but after every Choosing, the chosen Eaglets have to fly across the narrow sea between our island and the Philippine Eagle's island. However, one of your Eaglets was caught in a Human trap. Keeneye, seeing this, called us over and we freed the Eaglet, only to have another trap triggered, sending a dart into her heart. It was a pretty clever dart, so there was no evidence that it had been Humans, and our Eaglet's feathers were scattered around her. We were blamed."

I winced. "Ouch. But what do you want me to do?"

"Well," said the Leader, "Now that we've found Swiftwing for the Philippine Eagles, we want you to let her Aerie know her whereabouts, and explain about what actually happened to Keeneye the day she died."

"I could do that," I said. "But, um, what do I get in return?" Though it wasn't as if I really wanted anything, I still wanted to put on a mature face for the Philippine Serpent Eagles.

"You get to go free," said Dullsnap.

§ § §

It took me only a little while to get back to the Philippine Eagle Aerie, and by then, I had gotten over the shock of the day. The sun was going down, and I landed on the bent-branch tree just as the crickets were chirping.

I hunted a flying fox, and actually managed to catch it. I felt the satisfying sensation of sinking my claws into its flesh. *Not that soft*, I thought, as I pinned it to the bark and started eating it. The easiest kill I had ever done. After a satisfying meal of bat, I flew right into the main area of the Aerie.

Fierceheart suddenly snuck up on me and asked, "So?" I spun around and saw the rest of the Advisors spread out behind him, all staring at me.

"I saw Swiftwing," I blurted out. "I somehow managed to get captured by the Philippine Serpent Eagles, and Swiftwing was in a meadow next to their Aerie!" I paused for breath. "And you know how Keeneye died?"

"Yes, Hawk-Eagle. The Philippine Serpent Eagles killed her."

"Well, it wasn't them." I explained what had happened.

"Could be true," said Scarletcrest, raising her crest at Longtalon.

"Why would the Serpent Eagles do that, though?" asked Grayspan quizzically. "After all, you aren't supposed to fly to another Aerie's territory."

"Oh, it's part of their Choosing test or something," said Silverneck carelessly.

"Why don't we do that?"

"That's nutbrained. Only the birds with something that needs to be proven would do that."

"Alright, Sharpbeak. No need to prove your name."

"Everybird!" said Lightfeather. "Be quiet! Do you believe in Browntuft?"

"Possible," said Longtalon. "I mean, he has no reason to lie."

"Well, we all know that Browntuft is some nutbrained peace lover.

He could be lying because of the fact he wants no wars."

I glared at the speaker—Sharpbeak. "No, I'm telling the truth!"

"Yeah, totally. Totally, Hawk-Eagle. Peace is *everything* to you."

"Can you stop, Sharpbeak?" asked Fierceheart. "Either way, I am pretty sure that Browntuft is telling the truth. His motives for telling the truth are more than just simple peace loving. He's a simple bird, and I don't think that he would make up a scheme like this."

"Too bad Keeneye isn't here to tell us!"

"That's because she's dead, nutbrain." Of course, Sharpbeak again.

"Yeah, but it's pretty suspicious that we never found her body. The Serpent Eagles wouldn't have taken it away if they had killed her, but Humans might have." That was Lightfeather. I glanced at her and smiled.

CHAPTER 20

ENEMY'S LIES

Fierceheart took a moment to think. "Plausible," he said. "Plausible, but if you ask me," He narrowed his eyes. "I believe it."

Flying feathers, yes! Excitement coursed through my veins. I could feel my heart starting to beat faster. "But first things first, we need to rescue Swiftwing," I said. Fierceheart froze mid-preen, his beak halfway to his chest.

"That's right!" he said. "Let me see, who should we send? Highhead—"

"Had been exiled, don't you remember?" I asked.

"Guess what?" asked Fierceheart. "Highhead told me that you are working with the Humans," he said. "So either you're lying, or my trusted Advisor is. And Highhead's called trusted for a reason."

"Well, Highhead's gone, and for good," I said. "Why would he be *trusted* again?"

Scarletcrest said proudly, "Ever since my Leader cast the Ibon's curse on him, I wanted to check on him. So with the help of Silverneck and my Leader's permission, of course, we went to look for him. Once we found him, and he was still alive, we were about to leave when he called, 'Browntuft's working with Humans!' So then we brought him back with us."

I stared. "Why would you listen to him?"

"He told me that you would say that. Well guess what? He had a hunch, and it was right. You are working for the Humans, and he was the only one who knew. And Highhead's right here," said Fierceheart.

With a graceful sweep of his wings, he beckoned to the shadow of a nearby tree, and a faint silhouette walked out of the boughs.

It was Highhead.

§ § §

He sneered at me. "I don't give up, Browntuft. You thought I had been exiled? Well, like always, Browntuft, you were *wrong*."

"How are you even back here?"

"You see," said Highhead, and I could tell he was about to start a long story. "I told them that the Hawk-Eagle—"

"The name's Browntuft," I muttered.

"—conspired with the Serpent Eagles to help kill Keeneye."

And flying feathers, my mission was already off to a great start.

"Why else do you think they knew where we were? I tortured him and he told me everything."

"Hey what?" I screeched. "Hold on. That never happened! Highhead's lying! I don't work for the Serpent Eagles!"

Fierceheart only scoffed.

"Then how did the Serpent Eagle know Keeneye was there at that exact time? Your Aerie communicated with ours during that time, so you could have easily fed the Serpent Eagles information!"

I had no answer.

"You see?" jeered Highhead. "He has no answer, my Leader. He is guilty."

"In that case... How would you like to die, Browntuft? I never liked you anyway," said the Leader.

I panted in shock. Then my eyes met Highhead's, the cold, conniving excuse for an Eagle. I screamed, "I'm not a traitor!"

Before I could launch myself at Highhead, Swiftwing swooped in.

CHAPTER 21

THE BATTLE

Flying feathers, she was here! Crazy! Who would have thought that? "Swiftwing!" I screeched, but she was busy fending off her Highhead. Highhead's reaction had been surprise, then horror, then mild excitement.

Fierceheart spun around, his crest raising until he looked impossibly big. And then he saw the look on Highhead's beak, and then his own beak gaped open in horror. The Advisors backed off, and I knew what this was. A one-on-one duel, to settle the feud.

Like a Warrior, Swiftwing spiraled in the air then righted herself, all the while holding her claws out. How had she learned that? Usually, only experienced Warriors could do that move, and she was only two and half! And it worked. Her talons ripped through Highhead's feathers and flesh.

"Help!" Highhead screeched in horror and surprise as he dodged.

Swiftwing, her beak contorted angrily, screeched. She hit him with her wing and then raked his stomach, finally using her body to force him out of the tree. He collapsed into a bush, the leaves' pattern covering his mottled feathers.

Swiftwing turned to face me, ignoring the Advisors that scattered and her father who looked at us then flew away. Then she asked, "Is he dead?"

I didn't want to answer, but I did. "Maybe," I said, boldly. "He was accusing me of working with the Serpent Eagles."

"Good thing that I came in time, then," said Swiftwing. She forced her expression into something like the opposite of a smile. "Dullsnap told me you were coming here, and I was pretty sure you would need my help."

"Yeah, well who's the stalker now, huh?" I joked, "But, seriously, thank you for saving my life, again."

Swiftwing grinned. "Highhead is a traitor. But not anymore. He fell from a tree. If he's dead, at least he'll be accepted into the Ibon afterlife, but he'll most likely go to—"

"The underground," I quoted. Being in "the underground" was horrible, because you would be stripped of your wings.

"Where will we go?" Swiftwing mused, looking at me quizzically, "if the Poachers kill us all, Browntuft."

"The Poachers…" I had completely forgotten about them. "I wouldn't know. Flying feathers, we need to stop the Poachers!"

"How?" asked Swiftwing, slashing her feet across the branch under her talons. "It's not like the Ibon Spirit'll help!"

"I have a plan," I said softly. And I did. I had been planning for almost the entire time since I found out where Swiftwing was. "It involves talking to Humans."

"Tell me the plan," said Swiftwing. "Though I'm going to have to go back soon."

"When Althea calls you back—"

"You mean when we go back? I'm not going to be able to hear her from here."

"I meant that." My crest fluffed up in embarrassment. "Either way.

Then I'll trail you there. Before she can shoot or capture me, I'll talk to her." My voice got faster and stronger. "I'll make her believe that it's real, and we'll plan a way to defeat the Poachers. I can pretend to be the Ibon Spirit. I'll swoop above them and screech. Maybe they'll think I'm a ghost and run away. Got it?"

"I do," said Swiftwing, right before Althea made a bad imitation of a bird's voice.

"Kree-kree-kree!"

"Swiftwing!" I said. "She's here! She came to find you! We should go before any other birds notice."

"Time to put the plan in action," I said excitedly, scratching the bark in agitation. With that, I followed her back to Althea.

§　　§　　§

I soared through the trees, excitement pounding through every bone in my bird body. If this plan didn't work, I didn't know what would. But it would work! Flying feathers—it would have to! I felt like my senses had extended. I could hear everything, see everything now.

If it were up to me, I would have staged "the plan" in the Aerie, only Swiftwing reminded me of the fact that other birds were around.

I followed Althea's heavy footsteps as she ran around the trees. Finally, she arrived at the edge of the Aerie.

Althea stood there, waving her glove around like she was waving at someone. "Eagle!" she cried. "Come!"

I still wasn't used to being able to understand her. For a moment, I screeched in surprise. Then I remembered the plan, and I remembered that I could understand her. Althea waved and held her glove high. Swiftwing landed on it, sending Althea leaning over with the force.

Althea conferred nonsense with Swiftwing for a moment. Then she looked at the forest. And I knew that this was time. I landed on the floor of the sunny meadow, and started to talk to Althea.

"Althea," I said. Then I waited.

A few moments later, after a lot of screaming and jumping and pinching, Althea calmed down enough to talk. Her face was flushed red, and she was shivering. "You can't actually understand me can you?" she asked slowly.

"I can," I screeched. Althea gaped at me.

"Swear," she said.

"I swear on my wings," I replied, solemnly crossing my wings over my chest in a mark of promise. Althea squealed, getting down on her knees and chest.

"Why are you here?" she asked. Surprisingly, she was taking this pretty well, if you didn't count the screaming and jumping and pinching.

"Listen," I said quietly. "You know your friend, Jago?"

"How do you know his name? He's my uncle, by the way. Uncle Jago." Even though I'd never heard the word "uncle" before, I knew it meant the sibling of the parent.

"Well," I continued, "his group, the Poachers—" Again, a flash of astonishment on Althea's face— "they are killing the Philippine Eagle Aerie. They need to be stopped. Althea, can you help in any way?"

"Yes!" shouted Althea. She stomped her foot and pumped a fist hard. "I understand." She shook her head, sending golden brown hair flying everywhere. "I'd do whatever it takes to stop them."

"Then why are you listening to them?" I asked.

"Well, if I don't, my uncle will abandon me and I don't have any other family."

"Thanks for helping us anyway," I said. "Let's plan."

Althea froze for a moment. She stared at me, leaning on her elbows. I was pretty sure she was going to have imprints on her arms when we were done with this conversation. "Plan?"

"Yup."

A little while later, we got up, Althea rubbing her forearm. As I had expected, there were wavy grass patterns on them. Swiftwing hopped from one foot to the other in anticipation, and I raked the ground under my talons, churning the soil up.

Now we would only have to wait until nightfall, and then we could set the plan into motion.

§   §   §

While we were planning, I gathered some crucial information. The best was that I now knew where the Poacher's camp was, on the beach near the Philippine Eagles.

If I was correct, we would only have until the next Leader's Selection to scare the Poachers away, or else the Ibon Spirit would be angry with us all. Legend went that if there was no Leader for an Aerie, the Aerie would die. In other words, we'd better hurry. I started to pant, the dark forest menacing. If we didn't win . . . well, best not to think about that.

As I thought about the plan, we flew towards the Poachers' camp. It was happening, really happening, and this would decide the Aerie—no, the rainforest's future.

It was nearing nighttime now. We had some time to get there, set things up, and then wait. We arrived in the free space, near the small spring north of the Aerie.

I could see the Poachers' tents and lanterns as they got ready to sleep. There were a lot of whispered conversations, but somehow, I could understand them, even though I couldn't understand them before. Probably because I was actively aware that I was doing it. I saw Claudio, the grim faced one, stalk forward to the front of their camp. He placed his rifle over his shoulder, staring grimly into the darkening rainforest. Then he swerved and tilted his gun into the trees. Finally, he looked away.

Althea had said that they would have night guards, but that didn't matter, since I would be there and gone before they would see me.

Jago emerged from his tent and shouted something at Claudio, who nodded.

"Ready?" I asked, breathing softly.

"Yes," replied Swiftwing. She brushed her wings over mine. "You?"

"I'm ready," I answered. I took a deep breath, getting ready for the surprise. "Let's go."

I flew onto a tall tree. Then I swooped onto the next one, making sure that I could see well.

I screeched as loudly as I could. I whooshed over the camp, trying to make as much noise as possible. Flying feathers, was this going to work? My crest fluffed up. I didn't need to scare them, but I still needed to draw their attention.

Nothing happened. I howled, trying for a more threatening approach. I swooped lower, my wings almost touching the tips of their tall tents as I flapped and screeched. This time, the Poachers heard me. I heard shouts from the tents. Lanterns turned on, blurry-eyed Humans emerged from their tents, and Claudio's eyes widened and he held his rifle high. I almost laughed, but stayed silent. Then I screamed again, pushing with my lungs until my throat was hoarse.

"I warn you!" the night guard shouted. "If you don't leave, I swear that you'll die! Althea, is it you?" We didn't answer at all. The grim faced Human frowned as he looked into the forest, and his brow creased.

"Come out!" yelled Jago. "Seriously! Althea, come out *now*." When the only response he got was silence, he started to look worried too. He rubbed his brow, glaring into the forest. "Claudio, did something happen to my niece?"

"No," replied Claudio, backing away from the Poacher slowly. "I swear—I didn't do anything to her."

"Oh yeah?" Jago roared, punching him in the face. He might have been a bit overweight, but he was still strong. Claudio stumbled back, putting his hand to his mouth. He gave a sharp yank and pulled one of his front teeth out. I noticed that a lot of his other teeth were filled in with silver or gold, so it was obvious that this happened a lot.

Claudio growled and advanced on Jago, who I gathered to be the Poacher's Leader. He sucker-punched Jago in the stomach. Jago hunched over. When he looked up, his eyes were aflame. "Respect your leader," snarled Jago. "If it weren't for me, you would still be a ragtag group of bandits roaming the countryside! What kind of name is 'The Dirty Ones' anyway?"

"If it weren't for you," Claudio shot back, "By now, we would be rich! We already had a good amount just from stealing. And we'd only been in the business for a month."

"So?" asked the Leader. "Albert and Hubert are mine now. So are Gerald and Marko."

"They follow me," Claudio said, baring his teeth like a cat. "Albert, Hubert, Gerald and Marko! Who's your leader?"

The rest of the Poachers, whose eyes had been following the conversation like it was a battle, looked at each other. They shuffled their feet nervously, eyeing the two imposing figures. Finally, a slim, catlike one said, "Jago."

That was the start. After that, a bulkier one said, "Jago."

It was followed by two more answers of "Jago."

"Jago."

Claudio backed away from the group of his former friends. They advanced on him. As soon as Claudio reached a large log, the boundary of the Poachers' camp, he turned tail and fled, leaping over the branch and running in the direction of a human village.

I closed my eyes, waiting for the Poachers to get back to their beds. A moment later, the lanterns turned off. The bulky Poacher went to stand guard, pointedly staring in the direction of his former master.

"Now," rasped Swiftwing. I took a deep breath, then flew over the tents again, brushing the tops with my wingtips.

I screamed angrily, swooping around for another try. The Poachers opened their tents. Bright lights, lanterns, shined out, hurting my eyes.

Jago shouted, "Quiet down, whoever you are!" Then, unfortunately, he disappeared back into his tent.

The other Poachers looked at him. Then they followed his example.

"What do I do now?" I asked Swiftwing. She closed her eyes, thinking. She beckoned for me to come to her. I flew right next to her and landed on a branch.

"Keep at it."

I dipped my head and waited for them to fully go back to sleep. Then I soared above them. I beat the tents as hard as I could with my wings, screeching at the top of my lungs. "Kree-kree-keee! Kee-kee-keee! Kreee!"

Jago jumped out of his tent faster than I could imagine. He saw me swooping back towards the safety of the forest, and narrowed his eyes."A dumb bird?" he asked, aiming his rifle at me.

Swiftwing flew out of her tree, shrieking and screeching. She flew at Jago, and Jago's eyes widened. "Another Philippine Eagle?" he laughed, cocking his gun and leaning it against his shoulder. Althea's uncle squinted one eye and pulled the trigger.

Just before the bullet would hit Swiftwing, I flew in front of her.

I realized what I had done, and my heart started beating fast—only to stop, as the bullet hit me in the chest.

CHAPTER 22

RETREAT!

Black. That was all I felt and saw. I didn't even feel pain, just a sense of peace and warmth. I spiraled through nothingness, flying without my wings.

It actually felt good, to be what was probably dead. At least my last moments alive had been saving Swiftwing.

"No!" I remembered her screeching, right before Jago's bullet struck me.

I was dead, and it actually felt nice.

And then it stopped. I stopped floating through the nothingness, and I felt like I was falling. Just as I was about to hit the ground, a ground I couldn't even see but could sense, the fog surrounding my vision cleared. I wasn't floating in the nothingness anymore, I was in real life.

And real life, now that I was exposed to the nothingness, felt horrible. I had been too used to the peace of the nothingness. I uncurled myself from my balled position, only to find myself suspended in mid-air. I stared down at the floor, from high up so unnatural now that I wasn't flapping. The Humans rushed around, yelping. The peaty ground made me feel horrible, compared to the peacefulness of the Ibon Afterlife.

Flying feathers, what? How could I be in mid-air? I wasn't flying, unless I had been flying while I was dead, which was impossible. The thing supporting me gently set me down on the ground. I landed on my talons.

The Poachers stumbled back from where I had alighted. They looked at Jago, as if expecting him to act brave and fearless. Instead, he was also shivering, his eyes wide in terror.

I looked up, but could see nothing. "Behind you," whispered a voice behind me, and I turned to see Swiftwing pointing with her wing. I looked behind myself, higher.

Up in the tree perched a huge white raptor-shaped bird. It had a wingspan of at least twelve feet, and was six feet tall, from beak to tail.

The trees and forest filtered through the bird and cast shadows from the moonlight on the moist rainforest floor. As I watched, the ethereal bird flapped its wings once and rose above Swiftwing, the Poachers and me. It was so beautiful, so elegant...And, it was on our side. I bowed instinctively.

Flying feathers—I knew exactly what this was.

The Ibon Spirit.

§   §   §

I almost started screeching and jumping, but I forced myself to stay still, because if I acted immature right after being revived, I could tell this would break the atmosphere.

The Ibon Spirit. Here. Thoughts ran through my head and were dismissed. Swiftwing nodded at my surprise when she saw me gaping, my beak open in shock.

"The Ibon Spirit," she whispered, and her beak tightened. It was obvious that she hadn't forgiven it from earlier.

"I know. Flying feathers, it can't be!" I rasped back, glancing at the Poachers. They were still in shock, staring at me, and then up at the Ibon Spirit.

"What is it—that thing?" Jago gasped. He aimed his gun at it and shot, but the bullet only flew through the Spirit, sinking into a nearby tree. He cocked his gun and pulled the trigger. Nothing happened. The Ibon Spirit unclenched its talon, and the bullet dropped from the rifle.

"Yes," I said. "This should scare them away!" My heart beat in excitement when I thought about the possibility of the Poachers leaving the rainforest, once and for all. Swiftwing retucked her wings in.

"Maybe," she said doubtfully. She looked at the Ibon Spirit, still hovering above the Poachers. "Depends on what it'll say."

Just then, it started to speak:

"A brave bird's death has summoned me here, and I revived him."

"Flying feathers, that's me!" I wanted to shout, since I had died, but I kept my beak shut. All the Poachers jumped when they heard the Ibon Spirit speak. When it spoke, it gave off waves of comfort, images of prey and family and happy flocks. To the Poachers, it must have given off bad waves, because they all blinked in horror.

"This skirmish is over," said the Ibon Spirit. "You will leave this rainforest."

"No, we won't!" shouted Jago. He shot his rifle into the air, and even though it was no longer loaded, I still flinched. "Will we, my friends?"

"You're more our leader than our friend," murmured one of the Poachers.

The rest spoke up: "Yeah, we should just leave now, Jago." They walked to their tents to pack up. Just as they were about to go inside, the Ibon Spirit waved a wing, and the tent flaps blew closed. The bulky Poacher tugged at the entrance flaps, but they stayed tightly shut. They shuddered and backed away.

"This skirmish is over," the Ibon Spirit repeated. "You will leave this rainforest."

"How's it going?" said Althea. I spun in the tree and saw her grinning up at me. "I opened all the cages."

"Good," replied Swiftwing, glancing at the Poachers.

"All the birds have escaped!" said Marko, running with his arms over his head.

"What do you mean?" asked Jago. Then he glanced at the cages and saw all the birds he had captured flying out of their cages. "No!" he screamed in rage. "Who did it? Marko!"

"Your inner strife arises," said the Ibon Spirit quietly. "You will leave the rainforest."

"We won't," sneered Jago.

"Do I need to show you my power?" it asked. When the Poachers stayed firmly in place, the Ibon Spirit rasped a sigh. He held out his wing, and a gust of wind blew the Poachers back. Swiftwing met eyes with me, looking excited.

The Poachers stayed there for a moment. Finally, looking around at his terrified Poachers, Jago said the most beautiful thing that I had ever heard:

"Retreat!"

§   §   §

"Flying feathers, yes!" I screeched, louder than I thought I could. Beside me, Swiftwing smiled Shadow's smile, her beak lifting so high I couldn't see her eyes. "They're leaving!"

Jago ran to his tent and yanked a rope. The tent collapsed into a pile of fabric and poles, and the other Poachers' tents followed suit. They grabbed their guns, but the Ibon Spirit opened its beak and rasped at them. The guns twisted into knots and flew into the forest.

"Leave them!" ordered Jago when he saw some of his followers backtracking. "They're not worth anything for our lives!" The Poachers ran back to their village, yelling and shouting that this forest didn't have any good birds either way, why should they have come here in the first place?

Jago chanced a look back at the place that he had taken birds from. "This place has too many bugs!" he hollered, and then he was gone.

In the silence after the Humans had run away, the Ibon Spirit directed its beak to me. "You are a brave bird," he said. "Your former Aerie will know."

"Thank you," I said. Why was the Spirit complimenting me?

"You also need to go to your Aerie now, Browntuft. There's a danger there."

My smile shifted into a frown.

"And for you, Althea."

Next to me, I felt Althea tense up. "Yes?" How could she understand the Ibon Spirit? Maybe it could just make her understand.

"It was brave of you to go against your own kind and side with birds that you did not know. You may return to your village, but there is another option."

"What is it?" asked Althea eagerly. Her eyes shone in the darkness.

"You may stay in the forest. Unfortunately, I will not make you a home because while I can shift matter, I cannot make it, but I will allow you to make yourself a tree-house."

Althea gasped in amazement. "Please, please, can I?" she asked loudly. Be quiet! I wanted to say, but I was as thrilled as she was. A Human living in the forest with us would be new and strange, but not necessarily bad.

"Listen," the Ibon Spirit continued. "Not only will you spend the rest of your days in the forest, we also need you to bring good Humans here to help all the birds that are going extinct."

"I will, I will!" said Althea, her eyes shining.

"I can deliver stuff like palm civets," said Swiftwing. "And you can use fire to cook it!"

"She said that she'll deliver palm civets," I translated. Swiftwing sighed like she remembered that Althea couldn't understand her. "I can be the interpreter, and be your company. And, I don't know, find you a friend or something."

Althea swung her head around, looking at all of us. "I've never tried a palm civet before," she said slowly.

"Flying feathers, it's *amazing*," I promised, remembering the time when Swiftwing had hunted one for me. "I promise."

"In that case," began the Human, "I guess I can try."

"Where are the Poachers going to go?" asked Swiftwing, after a moment of silence.

"They might leave," I said, but Althea shook her head.

"I know my uncle. He'll stop at nothing to get back at us."

Swiftwing retucked her wings nervously, opening her beak to speak, but the Ibon Spirit forestalled her. "No, I felt his fear. He will not come back." Whatever Swiftwing was about to say was replaced with a rasped sigh of relief.

The Ibon Spirit turned to Swiftwing and Browntuft and declared, "Now, it is time for you both to return to your Aerie. They need you."

CHAPTER 23

FAREWELLS

Swiftwing and I flew as far East as we could go before we had to split up. As soon as the marks on trees changed, I halted mid-flight and landed on the tree that showed the signs of Swiftwing's Aerie. The signs were slashed deep into the tree, sap oozing out.

Before we left, Althea had told us where she had decided to build her tree-house in case we needed to go to her, and we had promised to meet her once every full moon.

"I need to leave now," I choked out, overcome with emotion.

Swiftwing met my eyes, then wrapped her wings around me.

"I'll see you," she said.

"Be safe," I said.

"You, too," said Swiftwing. Reading my thoughts, she continued, "Come find me if you need help."

I tightened my wings around her chest. "I'll see you," I echoed softly. Swiftwing gave me one last sad look, also full of hope for the future, though, and then leapt up and flew away.

I watched her retreating tail until I couldn't see it anymore. A heavy rain had fallen, shiny, dark green leaves obscured my vision. The ground was dotted with fallen leaves and little critters. I caught sight of a palm civet, but I didn't try to hunt it. With my heart feeling heavy in my chest, I jumped off of the branch, flapped my wings, then soared back towards my Aerie.

§   §   §

A few minutes later, I entered the dense grove of trees. Unlike many other Aeries, instead of choosing a clearing, my old Aerie had chosen a denser-than-usual grove. Silentflight, my Leader, had said it was because it was better for warfare and if enemy Eagles happened to come along.

I landed on a nearby branch, surveying my surroundings. Almost nothing had changed since I had last left. The Aerie was mostly empty, most of the Hawk-Eagles gone to hunt or practice fighting. As I flew to another tree, a flock of Hawk-Eagles flew out, alighting on my branch.

"And who are you?" asked the Hawk-Eagle in the front. Flying feathers—for some reason, she looked familiar. I had never met her, and she had strangely familiar wingtips that looked almost black, and honey-colored eyes that ended sharply near the beak, not rounding like most birds did. Because of her age, this was probably a practice flock—a flock made of birds that hadn't had their Choosing yet, but would most likely be Warriors—that had happened to find me.

"You're only a little younger than me," I said casually, looking around for somebird older I could address. "Don't I deserve to talk to someone older?"

The Philippine Hawk-Eagle held one of her talons out. "Answer," she said firmly. I almost rasped in laughter at the serious look in her eyes.

"I'm a Philippine Hawk-Eagle," I said slowly, cocking my head towards the strange bird, like she might answer me.

"I can see that," she snapped angrily. "Name?"

"Why should I tell you?"

"Because otherwise you might not survive the morning."

A circle of her flock surrounded me, but I wasn't too scared. After all, they hadn't even had their Choosing yet.

I rasped a sigh, pretending to be overwhelmed. "Browntuft."

"Browntuft!" screeched the Hawk-Eagle. "I've heard of you! Mother told me!"

"And who's your mother?" I asked, trying to sound languid and bored.

The familiar bird stared at me, her odd eyes probing my face. "You would know her as Oddgaze."

Flying feathers, Oddgaze? "I knew her, she was my mother's friend," I said, careful not to give anything away. "You're her daughter? What's your name?"

"She named me Blacktip," rasped Oddgaze's daughter. "If you come to the Aerie, I can tell you more about her."

"Okay, thanks," I replied. "Can you take me to Silentflight?"

"Finally, something I can do for you," rasped Blacktip. "Follow me." With a flick of her oddly-colored wingtips, she signaled for her flock to follow her, and led us to Silentflight.

§   §   §

Silentflight stared at us as we approached. He gave a start of surprise when he saw me, but it was instantly masked with disdain.

"And who is this?" he asked coolly, ignoring me and asking Blacktip. Blacktip looked at her talons as she landed on the Leader's platform.

"Name's Browntuft, Leader," she said meekly.

"Leave us now," commanded Silentflight coldly, staring down at me. "Now." I remembered the hatred that I had felt for him. I glared at him back.

"Yes, Leader," she finished quietly, and flew away, signaling her flock to follow her.

"What are you doing back here?" Silentflight asked, stretching to his full height, unfurling his wings. I stared at him fiercely, trying to forget my past.

"To get the Choosing that was rightfully mine," I said, the words coming smoothly from my mouth.

Silentflight half opened his beak in amusement. "What's that I hear? A pesky little runt begging for forgiveness?"

"I'm not," I said, forcing myself to regain my composure. I scratched the branch, and strips of bark littered the leafy ground underneath me. "My name is Browntuft, and I'm here for my Choosing."

"Choosing?!" laughed Silentflight. His Advisors flew over. "Do you think this runt deserves getting a Choosing?"

Oddgaze, who was part of the group, met my eye with a look of astonishment. A moment later, she dropped her gaze. "No," she chorused with the rest of the Advisors.

I was about to fly away and give up when I remembered the Ibon Spirit's words: *You are a brave bird. Your former Aerie will know.*

"I am not a runt," I said, stronger than I had ever spoken. "I will get my Choosing, no matter what you say, and I will be a mix, like Father, who was a Warrior-Healer."

"Your father *died*—" began Silentflight, but he stopped mid-sentence. The crashing of Humans was loud in my ears, near the Aerie. And then the low mumblings.

Then a spray of bullets screamed into the forest.

CHAPTER 24

RESCUE

I was not hurt. Though the bullets whipped through the air around me, I felt only the small disturbances of air as they passed near me. However, the noise had a horrible effect. Terrible bangs filling the air, deafening me, making me want to scream. But I did not.

Silentflight was not as lucky. Unused to the sound and feel of bullets, he screamed in fear and pain. Pain? Why pain? Then I saw it. A bullet embedded in his left leg, deep, too. His eyes were almost crazy with the pain. The bullets stopped, crashing into the floor and ripping through leaves and foliage, embedding themselves in trees, except for the one that hit Silentflight.

He thrashed around in agony, falling from the tree and crashing onto the ground. I dived off the branch and landed next to him, where he writhed and scratched at me. I had gotten multiple scratches before I finally kicked him in the head. He went silent and still. Finally.

I stayed there, panting as I got over the shock of being attacked by more Humans, and then began to worry. Silentflight couldn't die, even though he had bullied me and condemned me. He was the Leader! And I couldn't let him die because an Aerie couldn't be without its Leader.

I would have to heal him. There was only one thing—how?

Then an idea came to me in a flash.

I would have to find Althea.

§　§　§

There was a lot wrong with this plan. First, how would I get him to Althea, or Althea to him? Second, would Althea even be able to heal him? And third, would he die of the pain before I managed to get help?

One by one, Browntuft, I told myself. *One by one.* Getting him to Althea would not be easy, but I could probably ask for help from his Advisors. There was no way I could get Althea to come here; she was way slower on foot than a couple of Eagles on wing.

Althea, with the help of the Ibon Spirit, should be able to heal him, as well, and if I was fast enough, he wouldn't die.

I launched myself off the branch and flew towards the place I knew where the Advisors would gather again after the Humans left due to the incoming storm—the Leader's platform.

Once there, I didn't waste time. It didn't take long to persuade them, and soon we had built a moveable nest, which I had learned about from watching Shadow being brought back by the Philippine Eagles. We moved Silentflight onto it and soon were off to Althea.

As we flew, I couldn't help but notice how much of a downpour we were braving. The skies seemed to have fallen and let rain flood down. Very quickly, the Advisors and I were soaked, but then I saw Althea's tree-house, giving off a yellow light.

"Thanks," I said to the lead Advisor.

"Anything for my Leader," she said, avoiding my gaze. "Shall we go now?"

"Unless you want to make another trip through the rain, you

shouldn't," I said. "You will have to carry him back. Just find somewhere dry and wait for me."

"Althea!" I screamed. "Althea!" She must have heard me because she poked her head out of the window. Wow. I didn't know that the Ibon Spirit had helped her build her tree house so quickly..

"What?" she asked. The other Hawk-Eagles screeched in terror and flew off onto another tree. I couldn't help but smile. "Browntuft!"

"That's right, it's me," I said, growing serious. "This is my Leader, Silentflight. He got hurt by some Humans. Can you heal him please?"

I needed to give Althea credit. She didn't gasp, or stare. She only looked down, said, "Alright, and dragged the moveable nest inside. "Only, can you stay outside under the eaves of the roof? I need complete concentration."

"Sure," I said. Then I backed away and waited for the healing to begin.

§   §   §

I hoped the first thing that Silentflight saw was me. But what else could he see first? I was perched right at his talons, smiling like a Human. He screeched, swore, and finally calmed down. This was after we had transported him back to the Aerie using the same movable nest. We had waited almost three moons for him to regain some strength, and now, the Aerie Healers had allowed me to talk to him.

I tried not to look at his wounded leg, covered with some herbal paste, and instead looked him full on in the face.

"Brown—" he started, but I cut him off.

"—tuft it's time for your Choosing!" I finished, smiling. "Am I right?"

"Did you save my leg?" asked Silentflight.

"Yes," I said, a feeling of triumph working its way through me.

"Then I suppose you are right," said Silentflight grudgingly. "You earned it, Browntuft. You will be the oldest in this year's ceremony, because you missed the Choosing when I threw you out a year ago."

"It's fine," I said. "I can wait. It's my Choosing, after all." Then I stopped trying to act cool and collected. My excitement bubbled out of my beak in the words, "I've been waiting for this for a whole year!"

I'd gone through so many challenges. I'd been exiled for being a runt. I'd met with Swiftwing. I'd defeated the Poachers, witnessed them run, and finally, after all that, now I would have my Choosing!

CHAPTER 25

LATE BLOOMER

Iwoke up in the morning in my family's nest. It had been sort of falling apart since my parents were dead, but I had fixed it up. I preened my rumpled feathers.

"Hello!" I called without thinking to a Hawk-Eagle who passed.

The Hawk-Eagle looked at me and said, "Hello, Browntuft!"

"Well then," I said to myself as I finished my preening and spread my wings. I flattened a feather sticking out on my chest. "So...what do I do?"

I had only just asked that question when I remembered that I needed to wait until the sun was at its peak.

"I can do that," I answered. "I just need to eat..." I flew towards the outskirts of the Aerie, wanting to hunt something. My stomach ached at the thought of a juicy palm civet, but I was too small to lift one. I smiled ruefully when I remembered how I had gobbled down the entire thing upon meeting Swiftwing.

I couldn't help but feel a little sorrowful as I left my Aerie behind, but that was replaced with the excitement of the hunt. As soon as I saw a brown flash jump from one tree to the other, I was on the alert. I gazed around, landing softly on a tree, alighting so my talons wouldn't make any sound.

The cloud rat leapt again, chewing on the bark of the tree. As its black and white back faced me, I leapt and sank my claws into its neck, feeling the warmth of the blood. It jerked once, its limbs contorting, and then it was still. Triumphant, I picked it up in my talons and flew back to the Aerie.

A few moments later, I sat on my nest, feasting on the cloud rat. I ripped into its succulent flesh, feeling the blood trickle down my throat. I choked down a bone, feeling the fur tickle my throat on its way down. Finally, I finished my meal, scrubbing at the bloodstains aimlessly.

I checked the sun to see that it was almost halfway, the light half-blinding me. At the sound of the caws, I instantly straightened up, preening and trying to look better for the Choosing. A huge flock of Hawk-Eagles flew towards the center of the grove, and I followed.

I was the oldest Eaglet in the Choosing, and I panted as Silentflight called out, "One!" He was limping slightly from the leg wound.

I stepped forward with bated breath.

"Name?"

"Browntuft."

"Parents?"

I told him my parents' names.

"Yes," he said, dipping his head slowly. He passed his wing over my own, and I was frozen, as if shocked by lightning, for a moment. I finally relaxed my seized-up muscles. "You will be…" I held my breath in anticipation, waiting for him to announce my role. "A Warrior-Hunter. Now, I know this may be surprising," he said, not giving the audience any chance to argue. "But it is the Ibon Spirit's will. He will become a great Warrior-Hunter!" He spread his wings.

The ceremony continued, each Eaglet becoming their parents'

roles, with none being exiled. They were much smaller than me, but they appeared more mature than their age.

"That is the end of the Choosing!" he proclaimed, holding a talon out to the crowd. "I trust that you all will make our Aerie proud." He grabbed my wing as I prepared to fly away. "Browntuft."

"Yes?"

"I've decided to make you an Advisor, the youngest in the history of our Aerie."

I stared at Silentflight. I had thought that saving his leg had earned me a Choosing, but not this! "Thank you! Guess I'm no late bloomer after all..." I joked.

"Dismissed."

I flew to the edge of my clearing, and sighed. It had been a great, awesome day, yet it just wasn't the same without Swiftwing. I hadn't seen her in so long—almost an entire moon. What I would give to see her!

Then I saw the telltale flash of a brown crest behind me. "Here I am, wondering if you're going to need my help getting into your Choosing, and instead I find you as Silentflight's wingbird!"

"Swiftwing?!"

§   §   §

Swiftwing dropped a warm palm civet at my talons.

Flying feathers! Let's eat it! Was my first thought. Then I somehow held back from sinking my beak into it and looked up. "Swiftwing!" I screeched again in delight, and she matched it with,

"Browntuft! It's really good to see you again, you know."

"It is?" I asked, my shriek trembling in happiness as I asked my question. "I feel the same."

"Yeah, I had to pull some feathers to be allowed to come here," said Swiftwing. "Not that I wouldn't do it again."

"I would do it too," I said. "This is awesome."

"I know," replied Swiftwing. "Althea told me what happened to your Leader, and I came to make sure you wouldn't completely mess up. Congrats!"

I made a Human-like laughing sound. "Give Althea my thanks."

"I actually..." Swiftwing paused. "Unfortunately, I wasn't allowed much time here. I'm honestly going to have to be going. I'm really sorry."

"Don't be. You went out of your way to come here. I'm really thankful. This conversation was the best in my life. Well, bye for now, I guess."

"Goodbye," replied Swiftwing. She turned to the edge of the branch, looked back at me, and said, "Bye the way. The Leader's Selection is in a moon, and—"

"No flying feathers way! You're running for Leader?"

Swiftwing smiled. "You read my mind." And then she pushed off.

§   §   §

I flew back to my nest. Since I had gone through all my adventures, w normal life would feel boring. I rasped a sigh, leaning back on my s heavily. A Hawk-Eagle flew past. Instinctively, I said "hello." The Eagle glanced at me, and I recognized Blacktip.

e landed on my nest, then walked over to me and pressed against mth seeped into me. "Hello, Browntuft. I hope you made ne?"

d," I said, returning the formal exchange. Blacktip . "And you?"

he replied.

ied. "I don't like acting all formal. Do you want

to know about my adventures or not?" I had read her expression, full of interest.

"You guessed it," she said, squinting her eyes and cocking her head at me. "Can you tell me?"

"Promise you won't tell another bird," I said, glaring at her in mock anger. Blacktip crossed her wings over her chest.

"I swear on my wings," she intoned.

"Okay," I said. "But I need to hunt first."

"Alright." She put her talons against the nest and pushed off. "Can we share a small bird later? Oddgaze brought it in but she didn't want to eat it."

"Sure!" I called back. "At sundown?"

"Indeed," said my friend, looking back at me just as she started to flap. "See you later!" she swerved around a tree until it blocked my vision.

CHAPTER 26

A NEW LEADER

I could see Swiftwing forcing herself not to shudder as bird's heads craned over the crowd, including mine. She had come to see my Choosing, now I was watching the Leader's Selection. Fierceheart, the current Leader had let me in.

The Leader's Selection was far more significant than the Choosing because unlike being destined to have a role, this one was defined by one's own traits. I smiled Shadow's smile.

Next to Swiftwing was Sharpbeak but I got the feeling he didn't really want to be the Leader. I could see the two talking on the platform.

"The Selection of the Leader!" screeched Fierceheart from his perch. I stared at the soon-to-be-former Leader, majestic as he announced the Leader's Selection. "Today is a most important day, because without a Leader, the Ibon Spirit will not have a way to connect to our Aerie.

"We have two candidates," he shrieked. "We have Swiftwing, former Outcast, amazing Hunter, my daughter. And we have Sharpbeak, Warrior, son of Scarletcrest, Warrior and Advisor. You will hear their speeches and decide who you want to be Leader."

Swiftwing went first. I wanted to cheer, but held quiet as she started her story.

"If you know the rule that an Eaglet has to be its parents' role, then you will also know that if you break it, you will be exiled. That happened to me. Even though the Aerie exiled me, I still looked out for my Aerie, which is why, when the Poachers came, I returned to warn you all.

"The Poachers are—were—a group of terrible Humans that had only one goal—to capture the rare birds they could find. They also brought along Althea, a female Human, who ended up becoming our ally.

"I worked with Althea and Browntuft, a Hawk-Eagle I met who

had been exiled for being a runt from his Aerie. Together, and with the help of the Ibon Spirit, we defeated the Poachers, scaring them away. They won't come back for now. If I become Leader, I will abolish the law that exiled me in the first place, because regardless of each one's fated role, every bird still plays a part in the survival of the Aerie!"

Screeches and cheers filled the air, and Philippine Eagles leapt up, raking the air and flapping. Of course, so did I. It was a beautiful speech.

"Sharpbeak?" asked Fierceheart, his tone tinged with amusement. Watching the Eagles screech for Swiftwing, he rasped a sigh.

"I haven't done anything in my life compared to Swiftwing. I don't think I'm going to become Leader, but I still want to say this: Don't vote for me. I used to bully Swiftwing, call her a slowbird, a weakling. But now that she has saved the Aerie, I know that I was wrong about her. Please consider this. I don't care if you don't vote for me, but Swiftwing has everything it takes to become the Leader. She is kind and brave—she will lead the Aerie well."

My heart ached at his sudden change of heart. I had never heard the good side of him. I had always thought that he consisted of a sharp tongue and beak, but here was his good side in all its glory.

Birds smiled and shrieked in surprise and happiness, long keening cries. Even Fierceheart squinted his eyes in a smile and nodded at the crowd.

"If you would like Swiftwing to be the Leader, fly up." I flew up, flapping as hard as I could so I wouldn't be missed, my heart in my throat as birds flew up from their perches on branches. I waited for Fierceheart to count, and I realized all the birds had voted for Swiftwing. *Yes!* She deserved it.

"If you would like Sharpbeak to be the Leader, fly up." This time, following his wishes, no birds flew up. Scarletcrest herself had voted for Swiftwing, not her son, but Sharpbeak looked happy, not even jealous or angry.

Fierceheart's eyelid slid down slowly. "There is no need to count the votes," he announced. "Is it clear that Swiftwing is the new Leader?"

"Yes!" screeched the rest of the birds, me screaming louder than the rest of the Eagles. We all flapped our wings and shrieked. Sharpbeak was silent for a moment, then he himself started screeching, too.

"Swiftwing is a great bird!" announced Fierceheart over the crowds' shrieks. "She has proved herself twice over!"

"Glide!" shouted Fierceheart. Swiftwing sent herself gliding with one strong flap of the wings. I smiled until my eyes hurt from squinting. She looked so strong, haloed by the light and hovering. "Glide, Swiftwing, Leader of the Aerie of the Philippine Eagles!"

About the Author

Sophie Yao wrote this book while she was in 5th grade for her bird-loving friends. She likes to play table tennis and study mathematics. Sophie also loves to read and write. Her favorite authors are Rick Riordan, Suzanne Collins, and Leigh Bardugo. Her current favorite written form is poetry, thanks to inspirations from song lyrics by Lin-Manuel Miranda.

9 781956 380224